WHICH ONES WILL LAST THRU THE LAST DAYS OF ATLANTIS?

PERRY RHODAN—He sees the fabled island thru 21st Century eyes.

ATLAN—Specialist in cosmicolonization.

Khrest—The Ancient Arkonide.

Reginald Bell—Perry's pal, imperilled by a fate worse than death.

Pucky—The marvelous mousebeaver, trembles for the life of his friend Bell.

Homunk—A miracle of robotechnology.

Lt.-Col. Baldur Sikerman—First Officer of the spaceship *Drusus.*

Maj. Gunther Forster—Officer of the Earthship *Drusus.*

Maj. Van Aafen—An outstanding cosmonaut.

Capt. Rodes Aurin—Weapons officer of the *Drusus.*

Lts. Fron Wroma, Stepan Potkin, David Stern & Marcel Rous—Attached to the *Drusus.*

Dr. Arnulf Skjoldson—Chief medical officer of the *Drusus.*

Dr. Ali el Jagat—Head of the math dept. of the *Drusus.*

Sgt. Tomenski—Crewman of the *Drusus.*

Rico—A medical machine.

ARKONIDES OF ANTIQUITY

Capt. Tarth—Commander of the squadron flagship *Tosoma.*

Capt. Feltif—Engineer for colonial development planning.

Capt. Masal—Radio officer.

Inkar—Commander of the imperial battleship *Paito.*

Capt. Ursaf—Of the courier cruiser *Matoni.*

Commodore Cerbus—Leader of a cruiser wing.

Maj. Eseka—Weapons fir[illegible]

Umtar—Chief of coloni[illegible] il, Arkon.

Lt. Cunor—Remote contro[illegible]

Lt. Einkel—A fire-fighter c[illegible]

Lt. Kehene—Commander o[illegible]

Grun—A physics & math genius.

IT'S SINK OR SWIM ON ATLANTIS 8000 BC

PERRY RHODAN: Peacelord of the Universe

Series and characters created and directed by Karl-Herbert Scheer and Walter Ernsting.

ACE BOOKS EDITION

Managing Editor: Forrest J Ackerman

Translator Wendayne Ackerman

Art Director: Charles Volpe

Editor: Pat LoBrutto

Perry Rhodan

62

THE LAST DAYS OF ATLANTIS

by

K. H. Scheer

ace books
A Division of Charter Communications Inc.
1120 Avenue of the Americas
New York, N.Y. 10036

THE LAST DAYS OF ATLANTIS

An Ace Book by arrangement with
Arthur Moewig Verlag

DEDICATION

This American Edition
Dedicated to

STANTON A. COBLENTZ

Author of

THE SUNKEN WORLD

First Atlantis Novel
I Ever Read
(And Never Forgot)
in 1928

Fja

First Ace Printing: January 1975

Printed in U.S.A.

ORDER OF THE ACTION

STARDUST EDITORIAL
"Looking Glass to the Future"
Guest Astrogator
Greg Phillips
page 7

1/ RUNAWAY REJUVENATION
page 9

2/ CHLORINE WORLD
page 33

3/ THE KEY WORD
page 56

4/ TO LARSA!
page 64

5/ PREPARING FOR BATTLE
page 85

6/ ARKON DOES NOT ANSWER
page 96

7/ ATLANTIS—DYING
page 107

8/ DEEPSLEEP
page 123

9/ REWARD ACROSS MILLENNIA
page 128

THE SHIP OF THINGS TO COME
page 132

SCIENTIFILM WORLD
"The Invasion of the Saucer-Men"
Forrest J Ackerman
page 133

SHOCK SHORT
"Death in Store"
Dale Hammell
page 135

SERIAL
NEW LENSMAN
William B. Ellern
Part 2
page 137

COSMICLUBS
page 147

THE PERRYSCOPE
page 150

KRIS DARKON
Are You A Winner?
page 154

STARDUST EDITORIAL
"Looking Glass to the Future"
Greg Phillips

TOO INCREDIBLE for me. That's what I've mostly found a lot of science fiction to be and so I have read very little of this kind of material in my 15 years. Most books of this nature deal with unbelievable subjects, like millions of spaceships all over the universe, worlds inhabitated by walking trees and the like, and other such nonsense. So, when I first met Walter Ernsting (Clark Darlton) and discovered that he was a science fiction writer, I was impressed but not overwhelmed. His experience as a writer and, possibly, his seniority, were what made me first admire him; however, as we became friends, his personality began to take its toll on my science fiction skepticism.

The circumstances of the meeting, more than any other one factor, was conducive to my open-mindedness concerning the subject. My father had founded the ANCIENT ASTRONAUT SOCIETY to investigate the theories of Erich von Däniken and others. The Society was holdings its First Annual World Conference last April. Mr. von Däniken, one of the speakers, arrived with Mr. Ernsting and this is how I first heard of the PERRY RHODAN series. After becoming close friends with Mr. ERNSTING, I suppose out of respect for him I decided to read one of the RHODAN books.

The beginning of the book I chose (#41, THE EARTH DIES) was confusing but only because I was not familiar with the characters, and the story line was so different from other science fiction I had read. To my astonishment, it was believable! When I finished the book I was sure this was the best science fiction I had ever read. So I read another . . . and another . . . trying to catch up on what I had missed.

Now I've read numbers 26 & 32–45. Almost everything in the books is believable. For example, the thought of an astronaut meeting people from another planet is not so far out when you think of it. Some scientists hold that forming planets is part of the natural evolution of stars, and out of all those planets, some must be like Earth. It is only logical to assume that similar life forms would develop on those planets due to the similar conditions. Since some stars are older than others, some planets must be older than others. In the course of human evolution man's curiosity inevitably leads him to the stars and thus space travel is developed —on some planets to a greater degree than on others. This is precisely the situation in the PERRY RHODAN series between the Arkonides and we "Terranians", or Earth-people. So PERRY RHODAN could be, like other science fiction in the past, merely a looking glass to the future. Perhaps we should resume the moon shots; we might run into a couple of Arkonides!

1/ RUNAWAY REJUVENATION

A CELESTIAL ORB synthetically constructed by means of an unimaginable technology, it was a world without horizons.

Super-intelligent beings had built and established something here that forced an exclamation of wonderment and admiration from my lips during those first moments of my arrival.

Far overhead near the barely discernible defense screen, the glowing ball of an artificially created sun glided along its prescribed course. On the planet Wanderer, so named by Perry Rhodan, technological and scientific perfection reigned supreme. After having looked about in the various control rooms I realized that all the knowledge and skill of my own venerable race was meager by comparison, having been far surpassed by what I saw here.

An apparently ancient galactic people had immortalized here what we Arkonides had only hoped to discover someday. When I thought of Arkon, my distant home, I was overcome again with sadness, and yet upon closer self-inspection I realized that my longing and nostalgia for the tri-planet world of my origin was not as burning as of yore.

Slightly more than half a mile away from my position, the gigantic steel hull of a spaceship towered into the blue sky of this synthetic world, which had been surrounded by a mighty screen of energy. It was the *Drusus*, a super battleship of Arkonide design but constructed on Earth.

Nothing had convinced me more of the rise of the

formerly barbaric human race than this latest and most modern addition to the Terranian spacefleet. Its spherical hull was approximately 1 mile in diameter, exclusive of the equatorial ring bulge.

Perhaps it was this spaceship and other such examples that had allowed my longing for an eventual return to my home world to become less insistent. My long existence on the planet of humans had all but erased the impressions of my younger years. Memories of Arkon had grown dim and vague.

I squinted upward toward the synthetic sun and tried to consider by what technical wizardy the nuclear ball was being held in its circular orbit inside the bell-shaped energy field that protected Wanderer from the vacuum of space.

I thought of recent events with a shudder. Wanderer had been trapped in another time-plane by an overlapping of the 2 dimensions. The ruling intelligences of the alien universe had not wanted the artificial planet to escape and so it came about that the eerie collective entity of Wanderer had brought all the might of its technological powers into play. This had finally resulted in a transition-like hyper-jump out of the Druuf plane of existence.

Nevertheless, Perry Rhodan and I were mutually faced with the problem of locating this world which was no longer in its normal orbital location. In doing so we had to overcome physical phenomena that were incomprehensible because any logical approach to them was mind-boggling from the start. I felt inwardly void and burned out. It had been too much to experience, what we did in that completely unstable structure of semi-space between the 2 comprehensible dimensions. It had been a sheer accident that saved us and had served to complete those levels of energy which finally led to the stabilization of space.

My head reeled when I recalled the mathematical problems involved. After awakening from an abysmal sleep of exhaustion I found that Lt.-Col. Sikerman had already landed the *Drusus,* which had been waiting in the normal Einstein universe.

I glanced once more at the mountain of Arkon steel & plastic armorplate. From my position I could not take in the entire mass of the super battleship, as though I were at the foot of some cordillera whose peak lay inaccessibly remote in the distance. Yet this monstrous spaceship was astoundingly safe and reliable to fly.

The light throbbing in my chest reminded me of my biological pacer, a special cell activator about the size of an egg, which had held off the aging processes of my body for thousands of years. Ever since I had found out that Perry Rhodan and various members of his staff had received a biological treatment for cell conservation, I had been burning with curiosity. I still clearly remembered the day that had brought me the incredible gift from my unknown benefactor.

It had been long ago, almost 10,000 years by Earth chronology. During my wanderings through the various epochs of Earth's development I had almost forgotten to ponder the origin of my cell activator. But ever since I had been associated with Perry Rhodan the subject had again occupied my mind.

Curious parallels and points of coincidence in the course of events had come to indicate without any doubt that my own small apparatus could only have originated with the same mysterious being who had also given Rhodan a certain measure of immortality.

We learned just how much this "eternal life" was to

be interpreted as a relative quality when we strove desperately only a few days before to even be able to locate the synthetic planet Wanderer. It was there alone that the so-called Physiotron existed, in which the human body could receive the cell reactivation. This complex process was more simply known as a biological cell shower and in Rhodan's case each treatment remained effective for about 62 years. At the expiration of this time period, all those who had been so processed were required to find and revisit the Physiotron if they wished to avoid an immediate aging acceleration.

Rhodan managed to get there at the last permissible moment. He and Reginald Bell had entered the charging chamber's dematerializing forcefield when something happened that, for the life of me, I could not define. At any rate, rather than being a mere regenerative type process, it was exclusively the product of what had to be termed a perfected biochemical technology and which came as close as possible to the secret of life itself.

Most curious was the undeniable fact that I myself had never been forced to return to the synthetic planet at regular intervals in order to receive the cell shower. In spite of this I had not aged but had always remained at that stage of my existence which I had reached by the time I submitted to the influence of the small device within me.

Naturally I was in search of an explanation for this. I had come here in the hope that I might obtain fuller particulars from the ruler of the planet Wanderer. And in this regard the purely technical phase of it was a secondary interest. What seemed more important to me was the *why?*

For what reason should this mental entity have given me something that kept me forever resilient and young? When I wanted to ask these things of the entity, *It* had been too busy to answer. *It* seemed to have *Its* "hands" full with the task of rescuing Wanderer from semispace. And after we had all come through that crisis, *It* withdrew into seclusion. The collective being remained silent, as though *It* had never been interested in trifling with humans and Arkonides.

The gentle throbbing in my chest became stronger. A current of invigorating impulses seemed to flood through my body. There could be only one logical explanation:

The micro-activator must be a variation of the large Physiotron. Attuned to my personal vibrations it always seemed to take over whenever my metabolism and the processes of cell division became unstable. Since I had never been dematerialized, as was the case in the large cell shower apparatus, my bio-pacer must operate on the basis of carefully programmed stimuli which guided my normal life processes and corrected them as was required. I had not been able to find any other explanation.

I glanced at the special automatic watch on my wrist. Engraved on the watertight cover were the words: Made on Terra. The well-known phrase had always seemed strange to me. Everything I wore had been produced on Earth—even the Arkonide Admiral epaulettes on my shoulders and the insignia of my ancestral house had been made by human hands in terrestrial factories.

With these things my long period of wandering through the earlier history of humanity had come to an end. Rhodan, whom I had looked upon as an enemy 2 years previously, had become a friend. Now all that remained was to solidify this relationship and to prove to him that I had given up my plans of escape. I knew now that our ancient Arkonide Empire was under the rulership of a robot brain. Of course Rhodan understood that ultimately my allegiance was more with my people than with his but this was not cause for any disharmony in our relationship.

I had lived on Earth for approximately 10,000 years. Now the time had come to visit the place of my birth again and it was a foregone conclusion that Rhodan could be helpful in this regard. So it behooved me to help the leader of the Solar Empire to the best of my knowledge and ability—that is, if he still needed them at all! The state of Terranian technology was such that I was not able to offer much more to its science, although the earlier ancestors of present-day humans had once revered me as a demigod.

I leaned my back against the seamless wall and gazed across at the distant *Drusus*. They had grown big and powerful, these little barbarians from the 3d planet of Sol. I had been a witness to their awakening, their joys and sorrows and fears, their tragic mistakes and their quiet heroisms. They were now deserving of the leadership of this clear-sighted man who would guide them in the right direction.

A deep thundering sound tore me from my nostalgic reveries. Somewhere in the giant hull of the super battleship a gun turret had opened up. I saw the glistening energy beam race toward the sky. Far aloft its incandescent fire struck the impregnable energy screen of the synthetic planet and before the heated shock wave reached me I was already on the ground crawling for cover while groping for my MVR—my micro-video-receiver.

I pressed the activator button and waited for the green light. When it came on, Rhodan's face appeared simultaneously on the postage-stamp vidscreen—which meant he had deliberately placed himself before the ship's camera pickup, anticipating my response.

"Ahoy, Barbarian—what's going on?" I said into the microphone.

I could see his lips tighten in a tiny grimace. His voice emerged somewhat shrilly from the tiny speaker. "Nothing at all, Arkonide! That was the only way I could remind you that somebody's alive around here besides yourself."

For a moment I was nonplussed. Could it be that this gray-eyed Terranian had simply blasted off with a big heavy-calibre gun from the *Drusus* just to remind me to turn on my MVR? "That's a pretty rough way of tapping a friend on the shoulder," I reminded him reproachfully.

His laughter rattled the speaker. "That's a matter of opinion," he retorted calmly. "May I ask where you are at present? I've been calling you for the past 15 minutes."

"I've been close by, out here behind the main control room of the power plant tower, having a look at the distribution setup. Somebody around here came up with the idea of hooking up the defense screen generators with the hyper-sensor computers. The result is: if a hypertransition spacewarp takes place anywhere within a radius of 10 lightyears, the phase distortion triggers automatic controls here, switching the field output to maximum, which is about 10 billion kilowatts."

"Come again?" Rhodan's face seemed to reflect incredulity.

"10 billion kilowatt hours is the maximum output rate," I told him. "A nice current consumption, wouldn't you say? No, I haven't lost my mind. This planet may look like a cake dish with a cheese lid on it but it is a world of superlatives. I'm sorry your primitive intelligence isn't able to grasp it all."

We grinned at each other. Rhodan and I had developed the habit of ribbing each other once in awhile. I wasn't able to resist reminding him occasionally that his ancestors were still living in caves during the golden age of Arkonide development.

"Did you go on foot?" he asked abruptly.

The strange tone of his voice was a bit disconcerting. He must have been able to see me completely on his large viewscreen.

"Alright," he continued, "I'll send over an air glider from the *Drusus*. If you'll come over to the Physiotron chamber immediately, Your Eminence, I'll be much obliged."

"To the cell shower? Why?" I asked, almost breathless.

"I'm dispatching the glider," he answered evasively. "See you!"

The tiny viewscreen on my wrist communicator darkened. Rhodan had disappeared.

For some moments I lay there on the ground and stared unseeingly at the *Drusus*. Perry had acted very strangely. Something had happened—I could feel it!

I began to feel nervous. I thought of the bewildering effects of semispace and of Perry Rhodan who had entered the cell shower converter during an unstable axis shift. There had been no time to wait any longer. Without question, if we hadn't risked the cell-charging process, Rhodan would be a feeble and senile old man by now.

I waited impatiently for the disc-shaped antigrav glider, whose pilot would no doubt be able to enlighten me as to what was going on. However, I saw nothing moving on the steel face of the super battleship's hull. At this short distance I would have been able to see the bright spot of light resulting from opening an airlock.

I got up slowly and began to dust off my Terranian uniform as a matter of habit but it took a few seconds for me to realize that there was no such thing as dust on Wanderer, at least not in the vicinity of the few cities that *It* had built, more or less as a caprice. It was no great technical problem to maintain a dust-free environment. The tiny particles could be made to hold an electrical charge and then remotely controlled magnetic fields could sweep them up.

I waited tensely a few more moments until out of the corner of an eye I suddenly perceived a shimmering apparition. Not 10 yards away a small figure had materialized.

I was always somewhat at a loss when confronted by the paraphysical problem of teleportation. The ancient Arkonides had already known the principle of moving material objects by means of mental power but we had never been able to accomplish the feat ourselves. However, among Rhodan's mutants this complicated and mathematically ultra-dimensional form of paramechanics appeared to have developed into a sport. I had come to know 3 teleporters, 1 of whom was a non-human, and all of them shared a sort of fiendish delight in taking these so-called "jumps" through nothingness. If one knew how to effectively apply such forces of the mind, it became a convenient mode of locomotion or transference. As for myself, I'd never be able to get the hang of it!

With affected indifference I turned to look at the little 3-foot creature who, like myself, had not been born on Earth. Rhodan had aptly dubbed him "Pucky" because of the mischievous spriteliness in his big, shining eyes. He differed, however, from Shakespeare's immortalized imp in that he was a combination of a giant mouse and a beaver with a furry, spoon-shaped tail. The intelligent little fellow stood on 2 short legs which were encased in an elegant pair of custom-made hip-boots.

In addition, Pucky wore the pale green space uniform of the Solar Empire. Gleaming on his left shoulder was the insignia of a lieutenant in the secret Mutant Corps.

This comical-appearing character was nonetheless a sly one, obviously loaded with guile clear up to his floppy ears. Ever since I had come to know him, from the time of my flight to Venus, we had enjoyed a curious sort of friendship which mostly found its expression in cryptic remarks and subtle arguments.

"Hello, tattletale," I greeted him. "Would you perhaps be the 'glider' Perry promised me?"

The long mouse muzzle opened. I looked with fascination at Pucky's single, large incisor tooth, which he was fond of displaying at every opportunity. The non-Earthling's shrill laughter was painful to my ears but when it stopped suddenly I was startled. Since the time on Venus when I had thrown a piece of rotted wood at his head, I knew that he normally laughed long and heartily. The members of his race had an insatiable appetite for play. Laughing and fooling around were all a part of this characteristic.

The mousebeaver made a grandiose gesture with his hands. "I am the glider," he announced. "Give me your hand, spy!"

I frowned slightly as I watched the easygoing little fellow waddle toward me. To him I was still an Arkonide spy. When he was next to me I bent down and took hold of his arm without a word. He was light in weight, perhaps too much so for his height. Probably the creatures from the planet Vagabond possessed very delicate skeletons, which was certainly offset by the power of their brains.

Pucky's large eyes were fixed upon my face. His incisor tooth had disappeared inside his mouth. We looked at each other for several moments in silence, during which I sensed that he was trembling with an inner turmoil. He did not attempt to probe my mind by means of his telepathic gift. I had become accustomed for some years now to shield my brain behind a closed screen.

"What's the matter?" I asked. "You seem to be acting a bit strangely. Since when have you been satisfied to merely call me a spy? You usually have a few rascally comments to make, on top of your normal insults. So. . . ?"

I saw him clench his little fists momentarily and then he grasped my arm with both hands. "Do you know how the cell shower works? I mean—can you calculate its effects or maybe redesign it?"

His voice was shriller than usual. He spoke swiftly and with a surprising earnestness. The pressure of his little hands increased. The mousebeaver was very deeply disturbed.

"Well, the technical concept is fairly understandable," I replied cautiously. "But just knowing the function of a decomposition field is still a long way from comprehending the resulting biochemical processes. After all, I. . ."

"Hold on tight," he interrupted me. "We'll jump together. You have to get to the shower chamber. Oh gosh, I can hardly concentrate!"

I noted that he was extraordinarily pressed to achieve the condition he required and I asked him several times to tell me what was agitating him so.

"Bell!" he exclaimed, trembling in his anxiety. "It's Bell! He was in the cell shower machine when the phase-distortion started. Something's happened to him. No, wait—don't think so hard. You're sending out interference impulses. That makes it hard for a teleporter to transfer you. Don't think of anything—tighten up your defense screen!"

To me it seemed as if this whole accursed world were coming apart. On the one hand, Rhodan fired off one of his heaviest guns, and on the other hand here was unquestionably his most capable mutant, trembling with fear for Reginald Bell.

I conquered my nervousness and strove to screen off my brain waves. Moments later I felt a quick, painful tug. Pucky and I had made our "jump", as he blithely referred to the complicated process of building up a mass transfer field in the 5th dimension.

When I rematerialized I recognized the inner contours of the pillared Physiotron chamber. A tall, lean figure slowly approached me. In Rhodan's eyes was a frightening coldness. I had seen this look on his face once before when we had faced each other on a desolate world in mortal combat.

He came quite close before he stopped. "How good is your arithmetic, Admiral?" he asked. "I think I've run out of numbers." He stepped to one side so that I could see the cell-activation converter.

Close to the color-marked ring of the safety zone stood a young officer with a stubble of rusty red hair and a smooth, unwrinkled face. I had to look carefully to be convinced that it was Reginald Bell. Something seemed to stick in my throat. I almost staggered as I walked toward the danger zone. The man with the water-blue eyes did not move.

I searched for the deep furrows that had been etched into Bell's forehead during the past few years. The first wrinkles of care of course had appeared long before after his first Moon landing, which he had made in the company of the expedition leader, Perry Rhodan. On the 14th of May, 2042, Bell would complete his 104th year of life. At this moment it was May 5 of that year, so his birthday was only a few days away.

Some 62 years before today, he and Rhodan had both received their first biological cell shower on Wanderer. 5 days ago he had entered the Physiotron a 2d time in order to submit to the indispensable cell activation process.

I risked still another step before I stopped. This young man with the smooth, barely distinguished features—was this Reginald Bell, Rhodan's 2d-in-command?

"Reginald, is it really you?" I asked falteringly.

The full young lips hardly moved. His stocky, broad-shouldered physique revealed less fat around the hips than I had been accustomed to seeing.

"This is the way I was back in the 60s, more or less," he answered tonelessly, "when a certain Gen. Pounder sent me to the new Space Academy. At that time I was 27 years old."

A sense of horror welled up within me. Simultaneously I received a signal from my auxiliary brain, which had been activated thousands of years ago on Arkon. The message from its logic transmitter was short: *"Beware—breakdown during the 2d cell shower. Regeneration can be retrogressive. He is becoming younger!"*

This awareness was like a blow to the face. I struggled to hold on to my self-composure. My smile must have looked sickly, if anything, but Bell did not seem to notice it. I could sense that this energetic man had inwardly given up any hope of survival.

I turned to look at the others behind me. In addition to Rhodan, only the scientists and officers of the *Drusus* were in evidence. Dr. Arnulf Skjoldson, chief medical officer, stood next to Dr. Ali el Jagat, head of the mathematical department.

Jagat's thin, aquiline face remained expressionless as he handed me a sheet of synthetic material on which a line diagram had been drawn. Without preliminaries he

ATLAN

plunged into his explanation. Which I could understand becamse I sensed that there was no time to lose. It would have been purposeless to try discussing all the whys & wherefores of Bell's life and destiny. So it was typical of Jagat to call out the facts as he saw them:

"This is the first evaluation, Admiral. At the present moment Bell is at a stage which represents the 32d year of his life. Those pulse spikes show the beginning of the retrogression process. The flatter curves mark the time-lapse since the 2d activation. The chart is saying that an uninterrupted development of the process will bring him to a critical phase within about 60 hours. If we don't do anything to stop it, within 3 weeks he'll be a babbling baby."

The mental image of Bell as a flailing, kicking infant might have been amusing under less tragic circumstances but here there was no one who seemed to be amused in the slightest degree. The chart was the result of a test computer run and it didn't require a mathematician to determine when the critical point would arrive.

I looked searchingly at the doctor. Skjoldson made a helpless gesture with his hands. A mop of his straw-blond hair hung over his furrowed brow. "You have no solution, doctor?" I asked him.

"None! What has happened here with this equipment goes beyond my comprehension. I don't even understand the purely physical processes involved—and that goes for the biochemical changes as well. It is incredible to me that a maturely developed man should become younger. This goes against all the laws of Nature."

"Like everything else on this artificial planet," interjected Bell tonelessly. "OK, you can cut the chatter, men. No diapers for *me*. Before I get to that stage, count me out—curtains!"

His youthful face was grim. He looked at each of us, devoid of any hope. Finally his attention was focussed upon a tall, lean figure back in the entrance hall. I followed his gaze.

We had given the biopositronic robot the name of Homunk, which was short for homunculus. He was the product of what had to be considered an exclusive and esoteric science. He could not have been constructed more perfectly without coming close to duplicating the work of the Creator.

Homunk's biosynthetic facial film exhibited a compulsory smile. Beneath the virtually living yet synthetic tissue of his bodily "flesh" envelope operated a mechanism that had no counterpart in the known galaxy.

The fully positronic micro-laminar brain was more efficient than I had ever seen in the best of our own machines. In this highly complex computer brain there were more circuit elements packed into the space of a cubic centimeter than we could have stored effectively into a cubic yard and still get anywhere near the same performance. Its electronic speed was something like 80 million bits of information per second. How big the memory storage was we did not know. In any case, Homunk was something that one could designate as being perfect.

His builder-designer had fashioned him in the outward appearance of a human or an Arkonide. His speaking mechanism was a biological masterpiece. Using a positronic oscillator, it could convert electromagnetic control pulses into understandable and perfectly modulated words, with the help of its semi-organic vocal cords. Homunk was a walking miracle—but at present he seemed to be failing us miserably.

Rhodan beckoned to the robot. He approached with swinging, elastic strides. His stereotyped smile provoked me into making an unfriendly remark. "It appears to me that your great master has come to the end of his wits. Where is that creature and all of his roaring laughter now?"

Homunk came to a stop and his ersatz eyes looked at me. He called me "Sir", as he did everybody. "Since his escape from semispace he has not communicated, Sir. I am disquieted."

A cosmonaut officer from the *Drusus* laughed humorlessly at the idea of a robot being worried about anything. But then silence pervaded the large chamber.

At this moment I knew that the 2d catastrophe had just made its appearance. *It* had disappeared! The being in whom the mentalities of millions of disembodied intelligences were combined into a titanic psychic force seemed not to have survived the chaos of the return out of semispace. At the moment, we ourselves were practically the proprietors and rulers of the synthetic planet Wanderer.

Perry Rhodan only looked at me. He had apparently asked his decisive questions before my arrival so now he left the initiative to me.

Inwardly I began to despair. People of my race do not perspire; however, I felt a dampness around my eyes. My logic sector remained stubbornly silent. Apparently even my auxiliary brain saw no practicable way out.

Since my silence persisted, Rhodan interjected his thoughts. "Homunk has suggested that we reconstruct the entire experiment—and repeat it. Some weeks ago Wanderer was trapped by an overlap of the Druuf timeplane. Owing to the forceful method of its escape, the planet landed in an unstable intermediate dimension.

If we were to deliberately penetrate the time wall again and risk making an escape under the same conditions we would actually have to land in semispace. Circumstances permitting, Bell could then reenter the cell shower."

Rhodan's cryptic smile indicated to me that he did not consider the plan to be very promising.

I bluntly rejected the idea. "Impossible! How are you going to get the titanic mass of a celestial body like this through the warpfield?"

"With the powerful equipment available here we could generate a correspondingly large energy-lens to gate us through."

I made a negative gesture. It was senseless to even discuss it.

"Until something like that happens, I'm done for," interjected Bell calmly. "Atlan, do you have a better idea? I remember your work during and even before the breakout."

"He should enter the converter again and make an all out try to stop the process," said Lt.-Col. Sikerman.

I shook my head. No, that wasn't the answer, either. The problem lay in our lack of knowledge concerning the function of the Physiotron. While he was being charged, Bell had only been caught a short length of time in the distortion forces of the phase shift. We knew now that the existence of the planet in semispace had been a question of energy levels. Unquestionably the intermediate plane was related much more closely to the Druuf zone than with our own space-time continuum.

I only learned later that I had stood for more than an hour in a trancelike state in front of the perfect robot. The men of the *Drusus* continued their silence after I was awakened from my brooding by a painfully heavy pulse from my logic sector. I had found a temporary solution but whether or not it would stand the test of application was another question.

"You've arrived at something," said Rhodan. "What can we do?"

I felt exhausted. The mathematical problems involved were getting too big for even an Arkonide brain. For the time being I could only come up with general information. As I tried to look about attentively I noticed that my eyesight seemed to fail me to some extent. Rhodan came close, his face showing concern.

"You're still exhausted from your last effort," he said softly. "Can you still concentrate? I have a certain conceptual grasp of what's going on. Let's wait to see what your dice have come up with. Maybe our opinions will coincide."

I smiled at him and asked myself why I had ever considered this man to be my enemy. On Hellgate I had almost killed him. The humans associated with Rhodan reminded me more & more of the old Arkonides under my command who fought and suffered in the Earthly solar system many thousands of years ago.

They had been wonderful friends and rugged soldiers, as worthy of affection as these Terranians were gradually becoming. Reginald Bell for example was the personification of self-control. For several minutes now he had started to defy his fate. I could read in his eyes that he had determined to show no sign of weakness. Of course he knew only too well that with a continuation of the retrogressive process he would lose his high-spirited courage.

A simple concentration or contraction of his cell structure or molecular combinations could not be involved here. Had this been so, we would probably have seen his body begin to shrink.

But instead he became younger! It was something that I could neither understand nor express in mathematical symbology. Of the greatest secret in the universe, which was life itself, I knew practically nothing. I was a high-energy engineer and a specialist in cosmic colonization which also included the field of cosmopsychology. But I couldn't guess what was happening to Bell's cellular structure. Nevertheless I hoped for a miracle which might be brought about on the basis of a fleeting calculation in the field of probability.

I looked at the relatively small Physiotron. It was a columnar-shaped apparatus with a thick, circular platform. Farther beyond them I recognized several high-powered reactors, similar to all the others of their kind, which were in evidence everywhere on Wanderer. The cell shower's energy was supplied without wires.

"Are you able to service the Physiotron consistently?" I inquired of Homunk. When he confirmed this, I continued: "What power stations are required for perfect functioning of the Physiotron? What special circuits do you have to take with you?"

"Take with him?" repeated Rhodan with some emphasis. "Arkonide, I think you've hit on the same idea that I have. Keep talking. I'm all ears!"

Homunk explained the technical operation. It was relatively simple to understand until he came to the impulse converters, which had been built into the base of the apparatus. From there on my thinking capacity began to strike out. As for example I couldn't exactly visualize the process when the robot mentioned the creation of the stabilization effect.

A living organism also consists of atoms, from which molecules are formed. The principle of the Physiotron was based on a catalytic cycle in which the atomic agglomeration or cohesion is held stabilized and unchanged for about 62 years.

So it was clear in principle what had been achieved with the machine. The aging process of the cells had not been attacked at the cell core directly but at the infinitely smaller level: the atom!

After Homunk had answered my numerous questions, I saw things a bit more clearly. I looked at my watch. Then I stepped closer to Bell.

"Bell, until now I've only had a vague idea. What we will do is tear the cell shower and its power plant out of the foundation by means of antigravity beams. We'll have to be careful not to damage any of the mechanical installations. The combined operating unit will be mounted on a large freight platform, which we'll fit out with a vibrodrive unit. The *Drusus* will build up an energy lens-field that will be 1500 feet in diameter so that we can make an exit from normal space. We will penetrate the Druuf time-plane where we will try to synthesize or imitate the unstable conditions of semispace—which we hope to do through a concentration of energy inside a defense screen we'll have to erect. We know that semispace is an unstable condition or form of the 5th dimension, somewhat comparable to the unusable isotope of an element. An approximation should be possible but I'm still going to need every computer and electronic brain on the *Drusus* for calculating these effects. Are you in agreement with this?"

Bell remained motionless but he asked: "Looks like the operation will take about 4 or 5 days. Where in Druuf space will you get the energy for levelling the continuum?" He had grasped completely what the whole thing depended upon.

In this connection, Rhodan had also arrived at a solution. "We'll use another antigrav platform so that we can take one of the planet's major reactors with us. Homunk, can you arrange that for us?" he asked.

The robot calculated swiftly. After ½ second it replied: "In 12 hours & 14 minutes a semispace generator will be ready for transport!"

"Good Lord! What's a semi—?" asked Sikerman bewilderedly.

The robot only simulated a smile. It did not seem to be capable of any other human mimicry. "It is a special converter for supercharging an outer ring field—one that is warped in upon itself and closed so that 4th dimensional influences will be reflected from it."

With that we knew for certain! I gradually perceived that the technology of the collective entity was incomparably beyond our own.

"We can do it in 5 days," said Rhodan after doing some figuring in his head. "Maj. Forster, I want you to take charge of beefing up the propulsion unit of the antigrav platform. Sikerman and Aurin, you 2 get slidexes * busy on what strength you want in the mag-projector traction beams. Homunk will fill you in on the best way to break loose the equipment out of the foundation. Atlan, you and I have the small chore of making an overall integrated systems checkout. Let's get started." His tall, lean figure turned to go. For Perry the situation was taken care of for the moment.

"What about me?" Bell called out.

The Chief of the Solar Empire halted, turned to face him, leaving his back to the rest of us momentarily. "I've already spoken to Dr. Skjoldson. Until preparations have been completed, you will remain in the medical section's sickbay. A bio-chem deep-sleep shot will reduce

* Slidex: Mini-sliderule automaticalculator.

your physiological functions by at least 80%. It could be that your runaway rejuvenation process may be slowed down or held off by it while you're under. Skjoldson will handle all that. Alright, what are we standing around for?"

He was right. What were we waiting for? There was nothing much more to discuss. Pucky, that curious imp from the planet Vagabond, followed close on my heels.

"Want me to pop you over to the *Drusus*?" asked the little fellow plaintively. His big eyes seemed to be a sea of tears. It almost seemed to me that he was close to an emotional breakdown.

I bent down without a word and picked him up in my arms and in this manner the 2 of us moved toward the great, arched entrance gate of the Physiotron chamber.

Behind us a hectic hustle and bustle ensued. Sikerman's loud voice was unmistakable. Homunk, the perfect robot, stood motionlessly among the hard-pressed crew members of the super battleship, his synthetic smile still radiating its irritating charm and graciousness.

When I reached the open square in front of the building, Rhodan was just opening the door of a small pulse-glider. Silently he indicated the rear passenger seat. I came to a halt right next to him and looked at him penetratingly. In his case, nothing seemed to have changed. His body was as young and strong and limber as ever.

His smile told me he'd guessed my thoughts. "It was luck," he said. "I finished the cell-activation process at 17:24 on the 1st of May, so I wasn't hit by the phase-shift phenomenon. Bell didn't come out of the machine until about 19:30. The distortion effects must have attacked him during the dematerialization."

"We are aware of the facts," I answered reflectively. "But to me there's an equally important question: what's happened to *It*? Where is that collective entity keeping *Itself*?"

Rhodan's ironic laugh caused Pucky to whimper and cling more tightly to my shoulder. "That's Problem #2, Atlan. I guess you'd like a few words of explanation from him, wouldn't you?"

I nodded slowly. Naturally I'd be glad to find out why I had been furnished with a strange apparatus some 10,000 years ago by Earth reckoning. I felt the chest area of my uniform involuntarily. The activator hung there firmly on its unbreakable body connector.

"Let's go," said Rhodan, and there was an undertone of hopelessness in his voice. "I don't relish the idea of losing a friend. Or perhaps it would be interesting to see how far the retrogressive process goes. Where or how does it end? In the ultimate germ cell?"

It made me dizzy to think of such a possibility even by inference. One thing was certain: Nature had played a nasty trick on the biophysical processes of a highly developed intelligent being.

2/ CHLORINE WORLD

We knew more now about the interrelationship of physical laws in the Druuf universe than we had known months before.

At that time Rhodan had stood in bewilderment on various alien planets which had been afflicted by the unknown Druuf phenomenon. Although outwardly they had seemed to be undamaged and everything on the surface appeared to be intact, organic life itself was missing. It had taken a long time to postulate the existence of another time-plane from an analysis of the evidence at hand.

By now we knew that penetrating the superimposed continuum was merely a question of energy output. It was a plane of existence which was parallel to our own but with the difference that each universe had its separate time reference.

During the last expedition, alien life forms had been discovered which we had called the Druufs. But we still didn't know with whom we were dealing in actuality. The rulers of the other time-plane had remained invisible to us. Their robots and subjugated races had not been able to enlighten us.

But everything served to convince me that events I had witnessed 10,000 years ago were directly connected with present happenings. The time-rate differential made such a conclusion possible.

At the moment we were concerned chiefly with our newly-calculated law of reference points. Once a coordinating field was built up, it was to be deduced from this law, within 99.99% of probability, that a single dimensional jump would bring us out onto a planet within the Druuf time-plane. The materially stable mass content of the alien zone began to play a vital role for us.

The huge antigrav platform with its so-called semi-space generator had already disappeared through the circular ring of glowing energy. We had tied in 3 power stations from the giant *Drusus* to the warp-field generators. The energy thus available would have been enough to provide the entire Solar System with power for a period of 10 years.

Close above the surface of the synthetic planet, Wanderer, hovered that 1500-foot shape which we had variously named "lens field", "light ring" and "ring field". The expression "inter-zonal vector tensor and field alignment" might have been more exact, although even that did not seem to embrace the essentials.

I stood next to the lower wall of our largest transport disc, which was 40 yards in diameter. Made of light steel plate, it held the antigrav installation in its center. The 2 vibro-beam propulsion units that had been installed on deck did not have sufficient thrust for undertaking a long journey but in the present case it wouldn't make much difference whether we went through the ring at a pedestrian pace or with the speed of sound.

It looked as if the children of titans had been playing on the platform. Machines were lying and standing about everywhere, their massive stone and plastic bases torn from their foundation by pure force.

It had already become a problem to stabilize the fully overloaded flying platform. Mass was mass, even though it could be made weightless through operation of the antigrav equipment. At the last moment I had ordered the installation of a gyro-stabilizer unit so that we could at least have some assurance that our weird vehicle wouldn't flop over on us.

We had also placed the Physiotron in the middle of the platform and close by the high-powered reactors had been installed as the energy source. We had not been able to take along the bulky and complicated transmitter for wireless transmission of the power. The great hall of the cell shower now looked as though a bomb had exploded there. Rodes Aurin, the weapons officer of the super battleship, had gone to work with powerful tractor beams after Homunk had shown him where to unleash his forces.

When I thought about our jury-rigged conductor for handling a 3,000,000 volt potential, my hands began to tremble. Somehow the work energy required had to be brought into the cell shower's field projectors. Since we couldn't employ the wireless power transmission method, we had to fall back on the tube-field isolators of the *Drusus*. In my capacity as a high-energy engineer I had received the assignment to install the hurriedly-assembled power equipment and have it ready for operation.

Homunk had mentioned that the Physiotron alone needed about 600 megawatts at full load; an incredibly heavy power intake for such a relatively small apparatus. Whether or not the high voltage would be transformed properly in the incomprehensible devices hidden in the bases of the equipment, I could not be sure. Homunk had learnedly taken me to task, informing me that my calculations concerning the necessary insulations were illusory.

So it was not surprising that the antigrav platform seemed to be in chaos. Reginald Bell had taken one look around and merely shrugged. I could only force a small wretched smile to my lips but quite definitely I would not have wished to be in his shoes. Under these circumstances, to get into the machine where all these forces were to be let loose was more than a foolhardy undertaking.

Rhodan had turned on the gyro-stabilizers. After 2 minutes the heavy Arkon steel oscillating components had reached 200,000 revolutions. I waited in suspense, expecting them to fly apart, but nothing happened.

Standing silently beside me was Khrest, who cleared his throat nervously. I glanced at him briefly, noting that he appeared to be utterly exhausted. We had worked together for 5 days in order to come up with all the necessary data.

Rhodan weaved his way cautiously between all the machinery. When he came up to us he wiped the sweat from his forehead with the back of his hand.

"In spite of the deep-sleep treatment, Bell has gotten still younger," he said quietly. "Not at the same rate as before but the process hasn't been halted. The time has come!" Involuntarily he touched his lower lip with his teeth. "Atlan, are you sure this thing's going to hold together?" He pointed at the chaotic assembly of equipment.

"When I think of those power mains—!" I answered somewhat gutterally and left the sentence unfinished.

He walked slowly over to Capt. Rodes Aurin, who had a small special commando unit standing by to ward off any possible attacks. 4 small ships from the *Drusus* were also ready to go into action in case of any trouble. I had been hoping to keep these 200-foot ships and their considerable mass outside the Druuf-plane as long as possible. Even the powerful radiations from their propulsion systems and the weapons reactors was undesirable. It had been proved before that the time-ratio over there, unstable at its best, could change rapidly under alien influences. It was problem enough that we had to haul the indispensable big reactors with us.

Rhodan beckoned to me but I only nodded in return. It would have been senseless to mull over any further misapprehensions. These little savages from the Earth were about to show a former admiral of the Arkonide Imperial Fleet that they were more on their toes than he was.

I didn't feel well and Khrest wasn't much better. What was revealed in our expressions was something that was entirely undiscernible to Perry Rhodan. The Terranians undoubtedly had a younger nervous system than my own kind. For this reason we were equipped with other characteristics; at least those Arkonides who had remained mentally sound.

I listened to the thundering of the vibro-propulsion units. Everything on the floating platform was weightless. Nevertheless the 2 weak engines had to be held at maximum thrust to give us any forward motion at all. To me it seemed to take an eternity before we even reached the ridiculous speed of 25 miles per hour. Moreover, even this slight movement increased the wind resistance so that no higher velocity could be obtained.

We crept toward the shimmering light-ring with nerve-wracking slowness. Before we reached it, I took one last look around. Almost all of the Mutant Corps members were present. Pucky was already on duty "over there". He had been assigned to watch the robot Homunk. We had agreed amongst ourselves that this perfect machine was less concerned about Bell's life than it was about the composite being who was its master. The Druuf plane of existence was more closely related to the intermediate realm of semispace than it was to our own universe. Perhaps Homunk believed that "over there" he might have an opportunity to discover *It*.

At this close range the shimmering aperture in the void could not be encompassed by a single glance. When we were only 10 yards away from it, Rhodan issued instructions for us to close the pressure helmets of our spacesuits.

It was possible for us to emerge in an airless world or even in a place with a poisonous atmosphere. When overlap effects occurred and oxygen-breathing life forms simply disappeared, one could be sure that a breathable mixture would be found on the other side. It was different when one merely entered the realm of the Druufs at random. Of course the laws of mass were applicable; but they applied also to uninhabitable celestial bodies.

The transition occurred soundlessly. The leading edge of the platform simply disappeared as though it had never been there. As the energy field approached me I checked for my weapon involuntarily. At the same time I noticed that Rhodan also touched the butt of his destructive thermo-gun. I smiled. How much alike we were!

The crossover succeeded painlessly. The temporary flickering in front of my eyes ceased. When my vision cleared I could again make out the front part of the platform but the rear portion was not yet visible since it was still in the normal universe. I had to confess that this was the strangest transition I had ever experienced.

An alien world lay before us. It was as though some unknown force had set us down intact upon a desert island. It was a chlorine planet whose poisonous gases had been stirred up by a storm and which now attacked our unwieldy structures on the antigrav platform. Immediately our radio voice com deteriorated. We were no longer "at home"!

The platform began to sway dangerously. About 100 feet ahead of us we could see the glider which had carried Homunk and some of our men through the lens-field. I saw Rhodan jump to the controls of the gyro-stabilizer. At most the rpm could not be increased more than another 50,000 without exceeding the tensile strength of the whirling metal. The exposed gyros created the illusion of weird vortices in the glimmering haze. When I looked at my hands they seemed discolored and swollen. The small sun of this planet was a dim, greenish ball of light that was distorted in appearance due to absorption effects.

"This would be a great setup for a health treatment!" I heard someone say over the helmet intercom. It was Reginald Bell, who was bracing his legs to maintain his balance.

Suddenly everybody was shouting in confusion. Nobody had counted on this kind of wind turbulence.

I pushed my way through to the ship's chief engineer. Gunther Forster was struggling to squeeze more power out of the propulsion units. I could see his widened eyes behind the bullet-proof faceplate of his space helmet as I reached for the stepup switch controlling the 2 axial turbines. Forster had not taken the risk of using the present air as a medium of support and for jet action. Probably he had thought of the corrosive effects of chlorine gas and was also considering the return flight.

At the moment I didn't care whether the equipment could stand up against overheating by chlorine gas or not. Before Forster could say anything, the suction turbines began to howl. I switched the full power of the propulsion units' mini-reactors into the arc heaters and pulled down the control switch to the compression chambers.

Seconds later the auxiliary jets of the vibro-engines were spitting out superheated chlorine gas particles at a rate of some 12000 feet per second. Some of the men dove for cover but the immediate additional thrust in a forward direction quickly stabilized the swaying anti-grav platform.

Rhodan waved a hand at me but with the interference noises in the helmet speaker and the howling of the 2 jet engines his words were unintelligible. A hellish green abyss seemed to open hungrily before us.

It did not take more than a few moments before our previously snail-like pace had increased to an alarming extent. Homunk's platform became more clearly discernible. When we were within about 50 yards of it, I shut off the auxiliary engines. Nevertheless our surge in velocity was enough to carry us beyond the other transport platform, which had already landed.

Rhodan acted swiftly. The sudden return of gravity forced me to my knees. He permitted our floating deck to drop so swiftly that I saw us already smashed to the ground on an alien world that was hostile to life. He braked the fall close to the ground but our landing was anything but ideal. I heard the grating and snapping of breaking metal and equipment. Some of the sturdy hydraulic landing struts were partially bent and others broke off like matchsticks.

After we finally came to a standstill, the gyros idled down to zero. Only the howling of the storm wind still pained my eardrums. Our freight vehicle was canted somewhat on its side but the machinery installed on the deck did not seem to be damaged.

"Sorry about the crash landing so close to Homunk," I heard Rhodan saying, "but we were fighting a power drain during that maneuver." His voice came weakly over the head speaker and was noise distorted by heterodyning. "Is anybody wounded?"

One crewman appeared to have broken his leg. He

lay in my immediate vicinity and I could make out his pain-distorted features. However, he was the first to give a loud and clear answer: "Sgt. Tomenski, sir. Everything's OK—nobody was even scratched."

He looked at me imploringly, signalling me to silence. I smiled and helped him to position his injured leg more comfortably. A feeling of affectionate camaraderie came over me. It was not just for the sergeant but for all humankind. In their own way they were something to behold, these little barbarians!

The only creature present who wore no spacesuit in spite of the chlorine atmosphere was the robot Homunk. When I saw the stereotyped smile on his bio-face I could not suppress a harumph of distaste. Here in this environment where everybody was forced into the protective shell of a spacesuit, this human-looking machine appeared somehow to be a monstrous creation.

Rhodan jumped down from our platform. The local force of gravity stood at 0.95 g, which enabled us to move around fairly easily. I stared, suddenly benumbed, as I saw the clear impressions his feet were making in the ground. They had pressed deeply into the mosslike vegetation. At first I marveled that any kind of life at all had developed in this devil's kitchen but then I realized to my horror what had so suddenly attracted my attention to those footprints: how could Rhodan's boots have made such deep imprints? Moreover: how did it happen the storm whipped the vapor scuds past us so swiftly? Until now it had been our experience on the worlds of the Druuf that events transpired at a rate that was 72000 times slower than normal. Under such a condition the air should have been practically motionless and the vegetation would have to be as unresilient as steel.

This realization came like a bolt from the blue. Rhodan also seemed to have noticed it. He stood there as though suddenly rooted to the spot, having taken very few steps from the spot where he had landed.

With grim humor I called to him: "Well, Barbarian, is the expert stumped at last—or am I mistaken? This planet is subject to a time frame that's practically identical with ours. Events happen at just about normal speed. How does that tie in with your theories?"

Before Rhodan could make some response, somebody gave out a shrill laugh. It was Bell. When I turned toward him I saw that he was already opening the transparent safety lock of the Physiotron.

Khrest, the old man of my people, tapped me with his finger in dismay. In my agitation I waved him off, knowing what he was going to say.

Now the situation had become much more critical. If we were to come under attack we would not be able to take advantage of our faster time-rate. If the unknown enemy were only half as fast in his reactions as we were, it would be dangerous.

Rhodan didn't waste any words. Anyway, everybody had become aware of the phenomenon we were facing. Khrest had already withdrawn to the computer we had brought along. I was relying on this first-rate scientist, who was probably among the last of my people who were still undeteriorated in mind and spirit. Even so, he could hardly maintain that personal initiative in which we had excelled so outstandingly thousands of years ago. When I thought of my old cruiser commanders . . . !

It took a great effort of will to suppress the memories that welled up within me. The heyday of the Arkonides was past. I was a puzzling leftover from the old days, and Khrest, whom I considered to be weak and of limited vitality, represented the new kind of Arkonide.

Thus he belonged to the most capable representatives of the Great Empire.

Capt. Rodes Aurin didn't waste a single second. His loud commands rang out in every helmet speaker. 30 heavily-armed men of his special commando group jumped down from the platform to disappear like phantoms into the greenish mists.

3 other men ran back toward the clearly visible energy ring that formed the lens. Glowing brightly and only slightly distorted at the edges by light refraction effects, it seemed to hang suspended in the corrosive chlorine atmosphere. The 3 soldiers had received orders to cross the inter-zonal field immediately in one-man fliers at the first sign of danger, in order to alert the commanders of the Guppies that were waiting on standby for takeoff on the other side.

Owing to the interference effects of the lens, we ourselves were forced to operate at least 300 yards beyond it.

The next 30 minutes were devoted to our indispensable preparations. I took charge of the power supply for the Physiotron while Rhodan kept a strict eye on our perfect robot. Both platforms were so close to each other that their edges touched.

I looked worriedly at the 2 cannon-like power projectors by means of which our transport platform was to be inclosed in a shielding field that was to separate 2 continuums. The calculations were set; it was now only a matter of watching to see that the semispace to be simulated did not come too close to the real thing.

Bell was already standing in the cage of the cell shower. He acted calm and collected but those who knew him better knew that he was under tension.

After about 40 minutes I had finished my system checkout. I still didn't like to think about that main power line. It was possible that chemical processes in the chlorine atmosphere could make my high-tension insulations break down. The do-or-die safety factor allowed for an extra 500 amperes. If the breaker switches were to break down under a peak load, Bell would be utterly lost. During his full dematerialization, such an abrupt power loss could not be risked.

"Ready," I said over the helmet intercom, trying to sound as calm as possible. "How far along are you with your semispace generator?"

"Providing that it works—we're also ready!" Rhodan answered, somewhat hoarsely. "Bell, can we begin?"

Bell's voice sounded mild but carried a tone of unwonted gravity. "I'm ready for anything. And thanks a lot for all your efforts. Pucky, come on, little guy—let's mop up those tears."

Homunk gave me a signal. Both reactors showed a green light. I turned them full on. The surge was rugged. As though mesmerized I looked over at the blue-white beams of energy which had built up inside the contracting vortex compression field. This was also a form of power transmission but not as effective as that which had been under the control of our missing collective entity.

My insulation shields held up, although the 2 thermal converters were handling an initial potential of 3,000,000 volts. Whatever might be happening in the base of the Physiotron was beyond me to imagine. I had only seen some small leads connecting to the base terminals, so in all consciousness I hadn't dared to load them with more than 1000 volts at 80 amps. What they were receiving now and apparently conducting without any trouble must be virtually a ravening, primeval force, considering the size of the equipment.

Bell, whom we had just seen intact, suddenly became

a phantomesque shadow. A millisecond later all we could make out was a pulsing, reddish glow that took on a spiral form, seemingly suspended in the lines of force that had been built up by the Physiotron.

I was the last man to jump down from the platform and in a few fast strides I was at Rhodan's side. When I got there, the robot threw a switch.

A powerful roaring sound startled me. When I looked back at the cell shower it was hardly discernible. A pale spherical vortex had completely inclosed the antigrav platform.

It took us 5 minutes to find the right adjustment. When we reached maximum power for the 4D isolation screen, we were sure that an almost natural condition of semispace must have been created inside the reflector fields.

Rhodan looked at his watch. He seemed to be quite calm. "If everything works, we should be witnessing a phase shift. Probably everything will work out in the long run. He won't feel any of it."

From then on we remained silent. The special commandos were on the alert for any sudden threat and we found it quite a task to suppress our prevailing state of nervousness. Bell had to remain in the cell shower approximately 90 minutes. It was his only chance.

As the spherical vortex writhed slowly in its weird contortions, I could hear Rhodan's breathing become louder in my headphones. Homunk had charge of the Physiotron controls.

30 minutes later we had the visual impression that the formerly solid cell shower was as thin as a post; but from the side it seemed that the apparatus had widened considerably. This was unquestionably the effect of the semispace condition, of which we had been only too well aware, ourselves, but a few days before.

Khrest approached us in a state of agitation. His aquiline face was visibly tense. His voice sounded in our pressure helmets while the outside vapors kept condensing and crystallizing on our faceplates. I worriedly felt the various sections of my metallic spacesuit. It was not a pleasant experience to be working in a chlorine atmosphere.

Khrest communicated to us the readout results of the portable computer. According to his findings, the relative time-lapse ratio was 1 to 4.26374, which filled me with more alarm than before. It meant that our rate of movement here was only 4 times faster than that of a potential enemy.

The full impact of this figure enabled us to realize the true magnitude of the storm around us. The measured wind velocity of about 44 miles per hour must have been in excess of 175 miles per hour in the other time-frame! From experience we knew that our physical organisms tended to equalize the effects of these differentials. Why this was so could not be explained with certainty. Much more disconcerting, however, was the unavoidable fact that such a low differential as 1 to 4 could be found on any planet within the Druuf time-plane. This brought new and weighty mathematical problems into the picture which we could not get involved in at the moment.

When Rhodan had also finished studying Khrest's data, there was a sudden alarm. This came precisely 56 minutes after Bell had entered the Physiotron. Rhodan stiffened visibly as we stared at each other momentarily.

"What do you make of that, Admiral?" he asked me. "Were you ever in a situation similar to this?"

My auxiliary brain, which was practically identical to the photographic memory portion, signaled to me with a painful intensity. Again my abnormal urge to recount the past welled up within me. I suppressed the impulse and restricted myself to a hasty description of what I had done in a similar situation 10,000 years before.

Rodes Aurin called us. His face appeared on the tiny vidscreens of our wrist receivers, whose speaker outputs had been fed into our helmet phones.

"We have a hyper-sensor bearing, sir," he announced. "5 shockwaves all at once but no amplitude variations like you'd expect from a normal hyper-exit maneuver in Einsteinian space. We get fairly constant residual quanta. Looks like somebody were sliding out of hyperspace instead of just a straight jump—sort of calm and easy-going. And that, sir, is no ordinary space warp!"

Rhodan looked at me helplessly. However I remembered only too vividly an incident that at the time had meant the beginning of the end.

"Attack!" I shouted quickly. "Attack at once! Just don't wait for anything. The sensor indications are valid, however strange they may seem. Those creatures whom you call Druufs control a method of surpassing the speed of light which is different than ours. They don't make a transit jump through the 5th dimension like we do—they fly through it! Do you know what I mean?"

"Not entirely. To what extent do they fly?"

"They just don't make a hyper-jump in the true sense of the word," I said excitedly. "It was a puzzle to me at the time, too, until it suddenly burst on me. They conquer hyperspace in one long flight but a million times faster than light. Because of the different physical laws in that sort of para-void and considering the alien plane of reference there, it seems completely commonplace to them. By use of this system their destination star always remains visible. Also, they are not dematerialized as we are in our violent form of hypertransit jumps. For example, the Druufs pick out a specific distance they want to travel. Accordingly they figure out what multiple of trans-light velocity is required in the 5th dimension and their travel segments are chosen accordingly. It's pure flying but a million times faster than possible in Einsteinian space. In the 5th dimension the ultimate speed attainable is a billion times higher than possible in our universe. No, don't ask me how the Druufs come out of hyperspace. I presume it happens with a very short explosive shock but it's not comparable to our transitions. They simply go in, orient themselves and come storming out. The sharp spikes on our sensor readouts indicate this kind of shock wave. The more stable wavelines represent their approach speed. We'll still register a hardly noticeable jolt but by that time they'll be here."

"Aurin, does that check out?" asked Rhodan over the radio voice com. "Do you have any sharp starting spikes like that?"

"Yes sir, exactly that," answered the captain excitedly. "I think I'm getting an idea of what's going on. Orders, sir?"

Rhodan looked at me again. I was deeply disturbed. Memories assailed me more and more. My Arkon-activated extra-brain was merciless. Khrest placed a sympathetic hand on my shoulder. Since he also stemmed from a noble family, he naturally had received the dubious advantage of a government-sanctioned brain activation. Normal Arkonides had never come in contact with this experience. Only especially deserving and highly stationed people had been permitted to have the unused portions of the brain awakened.

Rhodan didn't wait any longer. Once Terranians have made up their minds, a variety of things are liable to happen.

Before I could properly collect my wits about me a series of flashing blue furies shot out of the lens into our view. I had been figuring on the 4 guppies on standby alert but here suddenly were all 40 fighter units—the full auxiliary complement of the super battleship *Drusus*.

I saw Rhodan grinning. Apparently he also was unaware that his efficient 2d officer, Lt.-Col. Sikerman, had taken the precaution to launch the entire guppy fleet. Behind the powerful 200-foot ships hurtled a pack of 3-man fighters through the light-ring—which made things all the merrier!

All crews on board the new contingents still had the advantage of a full-scale time-rate so for about an hour at least they would be 4 times faster than the most modern Druuf ship.

I went for cover as the pilots seemed to go mad, hurling their ships onto the target course at a horrendous acceleration. Searing hot shockwaves beat down upon us and the poisonous gases of the planet were gripped this time by a real hurricane.

There was a roaring and thundering as though the end had come to this particular world. The fighter pursuit ships continued flashing through the lenticular forcefield. It was our bad luck to be right in the unavoidable approach lane. The daring rascals pulled their noses up precisely above our position. The attack force consisted of at least 2 squadrons.

When the wild pursuit groups had passed us, Aurin asked anxiously: "Do you think that will hold them, sir?"

Rhodan's laughter made me catch my breath. There was something in his tone that dug at my nerves. He didn't seem to think the Druufs were at all invincible.

A few moments later he turned to me. "OK, Arkonide, we took you up on your advice. Bell still needs 29 minutes. That's how long our attack front has to hold out. What do you say our chances are?"

I looked for a place to sit down. When these Terranian barbarians became cocky and light on their toes like this it was usually a nerve-shocker for people like myself.

While I sat there silently, some crewmen set up next to us the hypercom equipment which had been "brought over" from the other side. The viewscreen was subdivided into 4 sections and immediately we saw the faces of the attack mission's commanding officers appear. Naturally Lts. Stepan Potkin, David Stern and Marcel Rous were among them. Apparently they were leading the pursuit ship formations.

"We have them, sir," reported Potkin with complete composure. "The hyper-sensors are operating. If they want to get at us they have to come out of hyperspace, so when they show their noses we'd better do something about it."

"That might be advisable," said Rhodan gruffly. "Based on our last encounter with them, a state of war exists between us and the Druufs. They've spotted us dead on. Apparently they've developed a method of detecting our lens-field whenever it appears. Such a force-ring probably causes a healthy shockwave in the 5th dimension. Get out into space and fan out into deployed positions. The approaching enemy units have to be held back at all costs. I still need exactly 25 minutes."

By now I had regained my composure. I was very familiar with the situation they were discussing. "Listen to me, Barbarian!" I interjected confidently. "Tell your men to close formation so that they can use their combined jets as a weapon beam. If the Druuf defense screens have not been changed they will become very unstable under hard radiation bombardment."

Rhodan didn't object too strenuously to this because I was giving him some of my 10,000 years of experience.

3 minutes later the Terranian ships were in the thick of battle. Over the hypercom we heard a crackling and thundering as 2 powerful fleets encountered each other. The pickup mikes in the guppies and pursuit ships transmitted the battle sounds clearly, which must have been unbearable within the echoing confines of the crew compartments. I recognized the familiar clang and clamor of weaponry in action as prolonged energy beam shots and closed formation broadsides were delivered. The noise was strongest coming from the guppies because the circular compartments of the spherical vessels were more resonant.

We looked above but with the naked eye there was nothing to be seen. The combat was running its course in the depths of space. Now & then reports came through from individual commanders. According to them only 6 opposing vessels had been detected so far. 4 of the long, slender ship types had been shot down already. There had been no sign of survivors but it was presumed that the crews consisted of robots. The 2 telepaths on board guppies K-18 and K-6 had not picked up any mental impulses.

"So much the better," said Rhodan, checking his watch. "Just 4 minutes to go and we'll have it made."

We waited impatiently but meanwhile I was wondering what Bell must have been feeling at this moment in the Physiotron. Probably nothing at all.

When the time was up and Homunk turned off the cell shower, we turned breathlessly to look at the nearby antigrav platform. The vortex screen disappeared. The outlines of the structure became more discernible.

Pucky had been standing close to me clutching my left hand. He suddenly squeaked excitedly and threw his little arms up. "He's alive!" I heard the supermouse yell out. "I'm getting his thoughts. He thinks he's only been in there for a second or so."

I ducked away involuntarily as the air suddenly shimmered. Pucky disappeared in a flash but instantly he appeared in the middle of the silenced Physiotron, where he jumped up and threw his arms around the broad-shouldered human figure there.

Rhodan and I merely exchanged glances. We understood each other without need for words. At least we had achieved one goal in any case because Reginald Bell appeared to be intact. To what degree the cell shower had reverted the strange rejuvenation process, however, was still an unknown factor.

Rhodan's eyes began to stare blankly. He was listening inwardly. Since I knew that he had developed a slight telepathic ability I did not disturb him. In a few moments he turned to me, slightly nonplussed.

"The mousebeaver reports that Bell seems to be completely himself again. The boyish features have gone back the way they were before. Do you understand?"

I didn't have time to answer him because at that moment a monstrous shape emerged far above through the dense chlorine atmosphere. Simultaneously we were contacted by the flight commander.

I saw the smooth, well-groomed features of Van Aafen appear on the viewscreen. As usual, the Major was cool, slightly reserved and pedantic. He was an outstanding cosmonaut who seemed not to have a nerve in his body.

"We have an alert condition, sir," he informed us. "A heavy enemy vessel has broken through the line and I am closing in with 8 guppies. I would suggest that you take cover."

His manner was such that he might as well have been

describing crumbled cookies at a picnic. We dove for cover!

About 1000 yards away something bright and glistening flashed through the greenish chlorine air. A terrible clap of thunder reached us along with a powerful shockwave, which hurled me several yards over the smooth deck surface of the platform. An infernal roaring sound became audible. Close on its heels a new cyclone struck us and this time I was lifted up violently. Apparently we were being just grazed by the vacuum suction of a fast-moving spaceship.

Things happened too swiftly for immediate comprehension. Several shadowy shapes went by at a considerable height above us. Bright flashes of light illuminated the semi-darkness and then afar off an atomic sunball seemed to inflate like a balloon.

Blinded by it, I closed my eyes and waited for what was to come. Somebody clutched my ankles, seeking support. We lay flat on the platform as the glowing hot pressure front of the explosion arrived. Like a world in collision. Minutes later I could not have explained how I lived through the inferno.

Almost benumbed by the experience, I helped Rhodan to his feet. Our 2 antigrav gliders had almost been capsized. The atomic blast had gripped them from underneath and spun them more than 50 yards across the flat terrain.

"That must have been at least 100 megatons!" groaned Rhodan. His left wrist seemed to pain him from a bad bruise. "Do you think these contraptions will still fly?"

"They've got to, sir!" said one of the crewmen. "All that equipment has got to go back—especially the Physiotron."

We turned to search for Bell. He waved at us from

the other platform. So at least all was in order in that department.

I was already checking the propulsion engines when the major's report finally came in. I heard Rhodan scolding him before I made out his words:

"Sorry, sir; that was apparently shaving it a bit thin for you. Stupid of the robot ship to explode like that. May I request further instructions?"

"The devil take you—and piece by piece!" retorted Rhodan. "You could have held your fire from the Druuf for at least 2 minutes. He would have been a few thousand miles away from us by then. OK, forget it! Stand by till we have these 2 freight decks secured. Then fall in behind with the whole formation. Use the pursuit ships as a rear flank protection. In an emergency the fighter jets can get through the lens faster than you could with your heavier guppies. Is that clear?"

"Completely, sir. May I presume to ask how things are with Mr. Bell?"

"You may," answered Rhodan in a more cheerful tone. "He was especially thrilled over that shockwave you sent us. Otherwise he's doing fine and you can pass that along to the individual crews."

Van Aafen's typical formality remained unshaken. "I'd appreciate it, sir, if you would convey to him my best wishes."

Rhodan merely chuckled but the repartee had only served to prove again what wonderful men and staunch friends he had on board his ships. 10 minutes later our loaded platform rose up from the ground. I guided it through the lens under full power, finally shutting down the auxiliary engines when the mighty curve of the *Drusus* loomed toward us from the ground.

Rhodan followed closely with the other platform glider. His radio dispatch had just reached the fleet squadrons. I was just opening my pressure helmet with a sigh of relief when the first of the guppies began entering the normal universe. That chlorine world had not been what you Terranians call a picnic!

25 ADVENTURES FROM NOW
You'll enter the errie
Starless Realm

3/ THE KEY WORD

Teldje van Aafen had submitted a very formal inquiry to me in an attempt to learn what methods were used by the old cruiser commanders of the Arkonide fleet for documenting their mission experiences.

At first I was a bit nonplussed but I finally gave what information I thought appropriate. Even a Perry Rhodan was not able to avoid the great battle of papers and documents but from experience he had always exerted every effort to mitigate this vexatious problem as much as possible for each and every one of his statesmen and commanders. At any rate, the 2d officer of the *Drusus* seemed a bit perturbed over his assignment to put every detail of his recent battle down on paper.

We had not suffered any losses, which was an indication of how much precision the Terranian pilots had used in their attacks. Of course their faster time-rate over the enemy had been to their advantage.

At the time I was busy making an evaluation of all the data that Khrest had submitted to me. Rhodan had temporarily postponed the return flight of the super battleship back to Earth because we felt obligated to repair all the damages we had inflicted in the cell shower chamber.

Since our return from the Druuf-plane, about 24 hours had passed. A robot army was engaged in the work of mounting the Physiotron and the power reactors in their former positions, including the appropriate power distribution hookups. A test run was to be made before our takeoff.

I suspected that Rhodan was still deeply disturbed

about the Druuf question. He knew as well as I did that the whole problem had to be settled eventually, one way or another.

A number of hypercom communications from Terranian defense and intelligence sources had been disquieting. According to these dispatches the terrible phenomena were still occurring on a number of distant worlds, of the type which we had not been able to stop. Entire races of galactic intelligences had disappeared over night. Huge planets had been practically depopulated. It was an occurrence with which we had long since become familiar but which we did not yet fully understand. What purpose could be served by abducting millions and even billions of thinking entities?

I had brooded over this question for some weeks now. An apparent solution seemed to be emerging in my mind but I still wasn't sure that my hunches were correct. The increasing tendency of our own time-frame to retrogress and slow up on the Druuf worlds appeared to indicate that a critical stage was being reached "over there". Somebody seemed to be making great efforts to cross-assimilate and equalize the different and conflicting laws of nature affecting both universes. Could it be that living organisms were necessary to this process? Was this the reason for the abduction of countless human and humanoid intelligences?

A few hours before when I had presented my deliberations to him, Rhodan had whistled loudly and discordantly in his reaction to what I had in mind. But now I was alone again in the main computer center of the super battleship.

Reginald Bell appeared to be completely back on his feet again. If one examined his face very closely there was still a trace of the rejuvenation effects to be seen but at least the weird process had been halted. Something had occurred in his more or less delicate cellular tissue that we couldn't understand but it was certain that a true stabilization had been reached, as was the case with Perry Rhodan.

Along about 12 noon I entered the great officers messhall on board the *Drusus*. The perfect robot, Homunk, had arranged to supply us with fresh vegetables. Everything seemed to be completely under control by now, especially since the Druufs had still not found a way to penetrate into our plane of existence. Apparently it was disproportionately more difficult to achieve an adaptive compatibility between the 2 continuums from their side, through use of a lens-field. Nevertheless something occurred that filled me with concern. I would have been happy to see us get away from Wanderer in that very hour.

I sat down at my established place and waited for the ship's officers to arrive. They filed in one after another with Rhodan and Bell arriving last.

Perry's tall, lean figure turned my way briefly as he nodded in recognition. During the meal he seemed to toss down his food absently and without enjoyment. As the automatic food conveyor system produced dessert and fanned out the individual portions to their proper places, he spoke suddenly to all of us:

"Pucky claims to have picked up some very weak telepathic signals a few hours ago. He says they could only have come from the collective entity—in other words, from *It*. John Marshall has confirmed this!"

My fork lowered slowly. In the messhall a sudden silence ensued. I looked across at the mousebeaver, who sat at the table next to Rhodan in his custom-designed highchair.

"It's true!" he insisted in his twittery voice. "*It* has been heard from!"

"And what was the import of the communication?" I asked with outward calm.

Inasmuch as Pucky's incisor tooth was concealed at the moment, it was obvious that he was quite serious. "The rest of you would not have been able to hear *It*—in fact the telepathic message was even hard for me to understand. *It* said that for a few days *It's* going to withdraw or go into some kind of state of retreat—that is, by *Its* own reckoning of time."

"*Its* time! Good Lord!" sighed Bell. "Do you have any idea how long that could be? We are told that *It* has a longer lifespan than the Sun. If *It* speaks of a few days but goes to special pains to add that *It's* referring to *Its* own frame of time-reference, we might as well just take off and forget about coming back for another 50 years or so at the earliest. By that time maybe by *Its* reckoning at least a couple of minutes will have gone by. You know I think I'm finally starting to get the meaning of the idea of 'relativity'."

I felt depressed. Again this time my curiosity was not to be satisfied. Upon closer analysis it was not so much a vague "wish to know" that motivated me but rather a pressing need in order to calm my sensitive nervous system.

Pucky's large eyes sought to bring me under their spell. I smiled and chided him for it. "No, little one—don't try it. I can't be influenced by suggestion. Did *It* tell you anything else or perhaps give you a message to deliver?"

"That's the only reason I was staring at you. *It* told me that the return of the planet out of the intermediate zone had caused *It* a lot of trouble. *It* seems to have lost a large part of *Its* psychic mass. Our experiment with Bell has transferred a part of the synthetic world into the same dimension. *It* could possibly return but for the time being *It* can't communicate any more. Do you understand that?"

Yes, I understood it, more or less. By "psychic mass" was meant the volume or size of its collective being. Apparently the abrupt breakout of the planet from the other plane had caused a weakening of the high forces of will and spirit which were ultimately responsible for the Mysterious One's tremendous powers.

I merely nodded. What could I say to all this? "Was that all?" I asked.

The mousebeaver looked across uncertainly at John Marshall, the chief of the Mutant Corps.

"Sir, we're well aware of how anxious you are for an explanation or some word of instruction from the entity," said the slender blond telepath. "So far as I could understand from that one short communication—distorted as it was by the signs of an overwhelming exhaustion—no particular information was received for you. That is, unless a certain puzzling sentence we picked up could have been meant for you."

"What sentence was that?" I asked excitedly.

The telepath communicated wordlessly with the mousebeaver. Following which I heard the exact wording of the sentence. It was probably typical for a form of life about which the only thing we knew was that it was an incomprehensible coagulation of countless intelligences.

Marshall spoke with slow deliberation. "The gift of the robot device was not entirely altruistic because even my own existence depended upon the longevity of one man who had found the weapon."

When Marshall had finished I thought I would sink down into the solid deck of the messhall. *It* had been aware that I was waiting for information. In spite of *Its* apparently great exhaustion, *It* had not forgotten to give me a hint, through the telepaths of Rhodan's Mutant Corps.

Perry looked at me searchingly. "Does it make any sense to you?" he asked.

Shocking surges of electrical current seemed to torture my mind. I felt that I could no longer revolt against the compelling impulses of my auxiliary brain. The surge of memory was too powerful. It was as if I were no longer on board the Terranian battleship but rather on a part of the Earth that had long ceased to exist.

Nausea choked me and my vision darkened. Marshall had spoken the key word that had triggered my photographic memory. I groped about for support until I felt a strong, steady hand under my arm.

"Is it hitting you again?" asked somebody worriedly. "Atlan, what is it? If you have a compulsion to speak, do so! What does the sentence mean?"

"My cell activator!" I groaned, plagued by a pulsating headache. "*It* endowed me with relative immortality in order to protect *Itself*. Now I see it clearly. I have defended the Earth—defended it with all I had at my disposal. At that time it was already apparent to me that Terra had become a focal point. It was comparable to a cosmic constellation that brought a temporarily stable overlapping of the 2 time-planes. The condition must have been enormously important for *It*. I received the gift of eternal life because of a coincidence. It's disgraceful."

Rhodan's grip tightened. My arm began to pain me. "Report!" I heard his voice faintly as though it were miles away. "Get it out of your system! It will set you free and we'll be able to learn something. I'll tie this into all parts of the ship so that everybody can hear you."

When I finally gave up all conscious resistance to the compelling impulses of my auxiliary brain, my torturesome head pains subsided at once. It was as though I'd been released from an oppressive curse of some kind and I felt that my very skull had let itself out to relieve the pressure.

Rhodan's distinctive features blurred before me. There was a formation of reddish rings from which the white-haired head of old Tarth slowly emerged. He smiled reassuringly at me and that was when my last sensation of pain left me.

My conscious mind had been shut off. Now I thought and functioned only under the control of my subconscious memory, in which everything that I had ever experienced had been identified and recorded.

I narrated in English, so I avoided giving technical data, officers' ranks and statements of cosmonautical distances and time, in Arkonide terms. These would have been incomprehensible to many men of the crew, since only Terranian leaders knew the Arkonide language. It also made little difference whether I referred to a first class ship's commander as Vere'athor or simply "Captain".

The last of Rhodan's words that I could more or less understand were: "You should think of how to tell us why it is that you are so well informed concerning the hyperspace travel techniques of the Druufs. Where did you get the information that they do not simply make transition jumps but move in the sense of flying? Atlan, can you still hear me? Marshall, call Dr. Skjoldson. He's as pale as a corpse. Hurry it up. Atlan, what is happening. . . ?"

I strove to produce a reassuring smile. My paleness was to be expected because the action of my logic sector interfered strongly with the flow of blood in the surface areas of my face.

I began to narrate. The present faded away. The past was the only thing that mattered now for my auxiliary brain. Someone approached me. It was Inkar, commander of the imperial battle cruiser *Paito*. . .

4/ TO LARSA!

". . .and so His Eminence, Imperator Gonozal 7 of Arkon, has decided to declare the system of Larsaf's Star as a forward fleet base for the Greater Empire. Atlan, Chief of Nebula Sector cruiser formation, Crystal Prince from His Eminence's House of Gonozal, is herewith bound and designated to defend Larsaf's Star with every and all means at his disposal and to take care that the non-Arkonide enemy is prohibited from invading the System. Further, Admiral Atlan receives herewith the personal order of His Eminence to promote the development and expansion of the young colony and to give support and assistance to the indigenous lower intelligences in that region, to the extent that they are docile and willing and take no precedence above military affairs. Signed: Umtar, Chief of Colonization Planning, Imperial Council, Arkon."

The tenderfoot cruiser commander was actually too young to carry such a position of military rank. Having read in a loud and clear voice the dispatch he had himself brought from the Council, he lowered the synthetic foil and waited. Outside on the new spaceport of Atlantis the fast courier cruiser *Matoni* was already on standby for takeoff. Capt. Ursaf had received orders to undertake the homeward journey as soon as he had transmitted his message.

I stood stiffly erect behind my work table. My throat felt suddenly parched. The overly decorative verbal flourish of these orders pointed unmistakably to the fact that they had been executed in the bureaucratic administrative offices of the Crystal Planet. For me the text of the dispatch was like a blow in the face.

Space Captain Tarth, my old teacher and now commander of the squadron flagship *Tosoma,* intimated his feelings through a malicious smile: ". . .support and assistance to the lower intelligences. . .to the extent that they are willing and take no precedence above military affairs," he repeated sarcastically. "Is that all they have to say to us? Where are the reinforcements of battle-worthy ships and materials we have been requesting? What became of the converter cannons, whose construction was only made possible through Admiral Atlan's procurement of the plans? On Arkon they seem to overlook the fact that Atlan's famous attack squadron now only consists of 2 ships. As for any invasion of the Larsaf System by the non-Arkonide Methans, it's entirely out of the question. We are 34000 light-years removed from the focal point of the defensive battle. The Methans have other things to do than to concern themselves with this tiny and completely unknown star whose planets have neither military nor economic significance. The costs of transport are higher than the materials to be transported. From a strategic point of view it's senseless to erect a fleet base here. Here there is nothing either to conquer or to defend. Aside from all that we lack the means of setting up the 3d planet and Atlantis for a repair station. We hardly have enough material to supply the few colonists who have remained with the most vital machinery for land cultivation. How are these facts to be reconciled with the pompous writing of a Council member who hasn't the slightest conception of the local situation? This does not speak well for the Greater Empire."

I made no effort to suppress Tarth's justifiable anger. It was a matter of truth that Arkon had written us off.

When I regarded this young Capt. Ursaf more closely it became clear to me how much the situation had changed in the stellar empire.

He belonged already to the war generation. He was the embodiment of the type of hothouse commander, hastily trained and force-grown, of whom it was hoped that he would come through his first battle unscathed so that he could perhaps benefit by his totally inadequate experiences. Statistics showed that only 8% of these men ever survived their first baptism by fire. On the other hand the Empire was no longer capable of scrupulously developing crews and navigators and commanders. For that one needed much time—and time was now a thing of the past.

The frightful losses in spaceships of all types could be swiftly replaced by means of full automation and robotization of mass production throughout the united star systems. But the thinking beings who were to guide these new fleet additions into battle had to be born first and after they matured physically and mentally they would have to be educated and trained.

Our losses must have been terrible. The war against the non-Arkonide methane breathers, monstrous creatures from the depths of the Milky Way, had already weakened the Greater Empire to a critical degree.

Up until 5 years ago I had taken an active part in the defense with my cruiser squadron. Finally I received instructions to restore order in a tiny solar system that was 34000 light-years distant. There I managed to remove an unscrupulous administration official from office and I sent him back to Arkon for the purpose of having judgment passed upon him.

Shortly thereafter I was again ordered into the system of Larsaf's Star because the colonists on Planet 2 had sent out a call for help. When I arrived and was forced to pit my battle-seasoned crews against an unreal, invisible enemy, it seemed that they had already forgotten that I existed at Fleet Headquarters.

At an earlier time this would not have happened but at present there were more important things to worry about. I evacuated the 2d planet when I found that our colonists were simply disappearing there. We had taken up a defensive battle but so far we were losing.

Uncanny creatures, totally unrelated to the Methans, were turning a tremendous natural phenomenon to their own purposes. In the course of months we learned that an incredibly rare process was occurring. 2 different kinds of universes, ours and an alien one, had begun to overlap each other in their peripheral zones. The difference between the 2 continuums was based on a differential of time-planes. It was the kind of relativistic phenomenon that we could hardly comprehend from a mathematical standpoint.

I had sent our settlers back home, for the most part. My cruiser squadron had been destroyed and now we were waiting for a decision.

I walked slowly over to the large windows of my workroom and looked down at the capital city of Atlantis. My former instructor, Tarth, had named the colonized continent after me.

I tried to get rid of the bitter taste in my mouth but I didn't succeed. The officers of my squadron who were present remained silent. They could guess what was going on inside me.

The courier considered it his duty to inform me further: "Your Eminence, the Empire is fighting for its existence. You wouldn't be able to imagine what's happening on all planets everywhere. The Fleet has taken an unmerciful beating. We have even been forced to take the colonial people on board the ships, which does not help the already deficient state of development. I was commissioned to inform you directly that it is impossible to spare the cruisers, heavy cruisers and battleships that you have requested. There is a pressing need for every fleet unit in the Nebula Sector. Under certain circumstances perhaps 10 light cruisers could be granted to you; however, you would have to furnish the crews yourself. The trained men of the transport command would have to be sent back to Arkon immediately."

I turned around slowly. Tarth's furrowed features seemed to be frozen. Inkar, the still young, hot-headed commander of the heavy cruiser *Paito*, had a sharp answer on the tip of his tongue but I waved him off.

I felt inwardly drained. "Am I supposed to fill our gun positions with a bunch of stone age barbarians from this world?" I inquired wearily. "I still have the squadron flagship *Tosoma* and the heavy cruiser *Paito* at my disposal. Both ships are only conditionally serviceable for combat because we were forced to make some engine modifications as a result of the incidents we experienced. We had to transform them into weapons because our enemy isn't vulnerable to normal guns. They should realize on Arkon that what's involved here is an intermeshing of 2 different time-planes. *Over there* on the other side there are alien intelligences. The threat posed by the Methans is concrete reality and comprehensible to the mind. But what's happening in the Larsaf Sector can affect the entire Milky Way sooner or later. The powers of Nature are on the side of the unknown opponent. In about 4 weeks, by local time Planet 3 will be in opposition to Planet 2. At that time we will be in the region of the so-called overlapping zone. I have converted Atlantis into a fortress. We have every prospect of success if we receive support in time."

The cruiser captain lowered his gaze. Naturally he could not take any position in regard to these things. It was absolutely senseless to present my arguments to him: he could definitely do nothing to alter the facts.

I came to a decision. "Ursaf, you will take off immediately. My report to the Imperator is ready. You are herby ordered to submit this information exclusively and personally to His Eminence. I do not wish to have this vital dispatch end up in some subordinate official's pigeonhole somewhere. If I have not personally received an answer from my revered uncle within 14 days, by standard time, I shall abandon the colony of Atlantis and return with both of my ships back into the Arkon System."

My rank was too high and fleet discipline was too severe for Ursaf to dare remind me of my obvious defiance of orders. But I could guess his thoughts.

Tarth's reddish eyes met my gaze somberly. He had understood completely. Naturally I would never give up Atlantis but it seemed that the only thing that would help here was a massive threat. Ursaf lowered his head and placed his right hand on his chest.

From my work chamber I could look out over the broad sea. Capt. Feltif, our capable engineer for colonial developmental planning, had established my administrative headquarters on the slopes of the coastal mountains. Far below me some quite respectable sailing ships were entering the great harbor that we had constructed. The indigenous people of Planet 3 were in the process of developing their own civilization.

I beckoned the courier to me and waved a hand at the distant scene. "It must be made clear to the Imperator what a shame it would be to relinquish the fruits of our labors here. We had to make a hasty evacuation of Larsa, the 2d planet. Including my ship crews there are about 14000 Arkonides on this continent. I have done everything within my power to face the expected catastrophe. Send me the spaceships and weapons we have requested. In 4 weeks the situation will be taken care of. After that I shall place myself at the disposal of the Empire with a combat ready fleet formation."

Again Ursaf said nothing. In spite of his youth he appeared to be well aware of what was transpiring on the distant Crystal Planet.

"I am even willing to refrain from *confiscating* your bright new cruiser," I added ironically.

The courier smiled uncertaintly while old Tarth let out a snort of surprise.

"A great idea!" he said enthusiastically. "The only question is, how would he get back?"

"Exactly," Inkar broke in gruffly. "It's a disgrace! We're lying here with outmoded machinery, inadequate port facilities and shipyards and a pile of junk from the stores of an evacuated colonial planet. When they furnished the supply depots there they weren't keeping the fleet units in mind. We are forced to make necessary repairs under the worst possible conditions. Tell that to His Eminence!"

Ursaf spread his hands in a gesture of surrender. It was purposeless to overload him with proposals and reproaches.

Tarth handed him the thin cylinder containing the dispatch for my worthy uncle. I suspected at the time that Ursaf would probably be the last military man that Arkon would send our way.

About 1 hour later I stood with my officers at the edge of the spaceport and observed the takeoff of the spanking new *Matoni.* She belonged to the 300-foot class and was equipped with a weapons complement which previously would have done credit to a battle cruiser.

With a dwindling roar, the spherical ship disappeared into the cloudless blue sky of the 3d planet. Throughout Atlantis the native inhabitants would again fall on their knees and raise their hands on high, chanting their songs of praise. To them we were gods; but it was very questionable whether these "gods" would be capable of defending Atlantis.

I looked about me in the circle of my officers. When it became known that the courier was to arrive, I had called them in from all parts of the colony. I was too well aware of their boundless disappointment to ask them for their opinions. These were the old trusted faces, although many of my companions were missing by now.

Commodore Cerbus, leader of my cruiser wing, had fallen in a defensive battle at least a year ago. With him more than 40 other commanders and 10,000 top-rate specialists had lost their lives.

What sense did it make to defend a solar system, named after a discoverer called Larsaf—against an uncanny enemy? We didn't know who we were fighting.

Then there were still other things that had bewildered us. Shortly after the difficult battle on the 2d planet, a robot handed me a small device the size of an egg. According to instructions I was to carry it always against my chest, close to the heart.

Where the robot ship came from I wasn't able to learn. Ostensibly the mysterious stimuli from the so-called "activator" were supposed to make me relatively immortal. I couldn't quite believe the communications of a complex machine whose builder-designer only made his presence known by loud laughter. Nevertheless, I continued to carry the hollow metallic container close to my chest as instructed. Whether it actually hindered my natural aging processes or suspended them completely I had not been able to determine over such a short time span. At any rate I felt as young, fresh and limber as ever.

My purely personal problem also didn't seem to be so important any more. Here was involved the existence of 14000 Arkonides, several million natives and a young but wonderful colony.

Atlantis was an island continent which was approximately 1200 miles in length. The tropical climate and the clear air at higher altitudes was very pleasing to us. In the course of 4 years we had created a model colony here—and we had also imparted a few skills to the brown-skinned peoples on the large continents to the West and East of Atlantis.

I had appointed Inkar to be Chief of the Western Land. In a mood of cheerful amusement he reported to me that the natives there had elevated him to a kind of god-king. They simply called him "Inka"—and the sun symbol of my venerable family was chosen as a symbol of divinity.

More than 500 of my soldiers and settlers had asked for permission to marry during the past year. I had granted all such requests because I couldn't see why my people had to suffer more loneliness on this lost outpost than the situation otherwise required.

The married couples seemed to be quite happy although Tarth kept reminding me that I had actually violated colonial law. Intelligent beings of development stage B were not supposed to intermarry with Arkonides. I had invoked the Emergency Powers Act and drawn the attention of all native women to the separation clause. According to the decision of the Colonization Board, marriages between Arkonides and primitive colonists were to be considered ineffectual and void whenever the husband was required to leave the planet concerned.

This was why I hoped to be able to repel the sinister enemy from the depths of another time-plane so that I could preserve this new home for my colonists. In this particular case an intermingling of the Arkonide-like natives was permitted and even practiced. Unions between Arkonides and the female members of an alien race were tolerated, in any case. But our men were obligated to educate their wives and to raise their eventual offspring in accordance with our advanced culture and technology. This was how new peoples and cultures were developed. I didn't see why I shouldn't be magnanimous.

If a battle-tested fleet admiral is assigned responsibility for administering an entire planet, then he should be granted the greatest possible freedom of decision.

A loud howling sound brought me back into present reality. A 200-foot auxiliary flier from the battleship *Tosoma* was coming in for a landing.

"I think he's lost his mind!" shouted Tarth incredulously.

In the next moment I was on the ground with my staff officers, going for cover. I waited until the hot shockwave had blasted over us. When I raised my head I saw that the ship was reeling uncertainly. It finally crashed to the ground near the mighty hull of the *Tosoma*. I noticed that it was the TO-4, whose commander had been assigned by me to make a reconnaissance flight near the orbit of the 2d planet.

3 of the sturdy landing struts had been crumpled by the jolt, which indicated that the antigrav hadn't been functioning properly. The ship had made an old-fash-

ioned landing on its radiation jets, if such a near crash could actually be called a landing. The TO-4 lay just about 1000 yards from us.

As if coming out of a trance, I looked across at the scene of the accident. The whine of a ground-glider engine brought me back to a state of alertness. Tarth and Inkar were already seated in the open vehicle. I got up without a word and jumped over the door panel. Our driver got underway at once. Before we could say a word we were racing over the flat surface of the spaceport.

Tarth's face was grim. When we finally became aware of the giant, blistered shot hole in the solid hull of the ship, we knew why the crew had elected to make such a wild landing. From the lower cargo lock of the 2500-foot *Tosoma*, the steel figures of salvage robots were already emerging. There appeared to be a fire inside the damaged spacecraft, as evidenced by the thick, oily black clouds of smoke.

When we came to a stop, Inkar spoke in a flat tone of voice: "That's a thermal hit, no question about it. In the name of the Greater Empire, who could have done that to the ship?"

I was already running toward the canted hull. Swiftly moving robots were moving in through the open airlocks. In spite of this it took several minutes before they appeared with the first survivors. The TO-4 had a crew of 15 men.

We waited in silence until the machines had completed their work. The fire-fighting equipment of the *Tosoma* was also brought into action. The fire in power room #2 of the flier was finally quenched. Only 11 crewmen were brought out. 3 of them were dead and almost all of the others were wounded.

I waited until the chief medical officer of the *Tosoma*

called me. Lt. Kehene, commander of the TO-4, had suffered severe burns but was no longer in pain. A plasma bath would soon heal his wounds. I would soon be able to question him without too much risk.

I kneeled down next to the stretcher and slipped off my bothersome shoulder cape. I had a long experience in having to face men in such a condition as this. In an age of energy weapons, burns of every type by far outweighed all other kinds of injuries.

Kehene was breathing hard but could speak. "TO-4, Your Eminence, returned from patrol flight. There was a relative-energy front over the 2d planet. I took up the prescribed picket point, to keep the required security distance, and all I did was observe. This time the relative velocity in the other time-plane checked out at almost 30 miles per second, which was considerably faster than usual. I was measuring the inter-zonal points when suddenly this hole appeared in empty space."

A medico interrupted us long enough to give him another pain-relieving injection. The synthetic material of Kehene's uniform was sticking in places to his burned flesh. But my mind held to his amazing information. A hole in empty space?

The young commander reaffirmed it. "That's what it was, Eminence. It looked like a giant funnel, opening wider and wider. It opened at about 10% of the real-time speed of light, and behind it the stars disappeared. Instead, the space it covered had a deep reddish glow with darker spots here & there inside it. The space-shock instruments were just starting to show some short-burst hyper-warps when all of a sudden they were on top of us."

Tarth was beside me and now he grunted fiercely: "*Who* was on top of you?"

"There were 4 unidentified spaceships—cylinder-shaped. Our energy detectors indicated radiant propulsion. We were getting true hyper-blips on the registers so I knew we weren't dealing with any disembodied phantoms this time. The 4 ships were coming out of the funnel. I pulled back right away at full retro-power but they had the speed advantage over us. I mean we were still like sitting ducks at the picket point while they were already at about half light speed. They opened fire with thermo-cannons, which have about the same effect as our impulse-projectors. My evasion course was locked to the hit-probability logic of the energy-detection positronicon. I was able to dodge their combined salvos 3 times but they finally got in an angle shot on one of my pullout curves. The TO-4 was heavily hit near the ring-skirt zone. My antigravs went out along with the radio and engines 1 & 3. I wouldn't have made it out of there if the 3 remaining ships hadn't suddenly gone back into their funnel. As I flew away the whole apparition disappeared. The return flight and the landing were a tough go, Your Eminence. Half the crew is knocked out."

Kehene closed his eyes. Shortly thereafter he was taken away to the ship's sickbay on board the *Tosoma.* We watched the robot medicos until they and the wounded patient had disappeared into the ground entrance lock.

The technical crew from the flagship was already inside the wreck, which was all we could call our priceless auxiliary flier now. The *Tosoma* had only had 4 of them on board and the TO-4 had been the only one of them that was still intact.

I remembered the physical and mathematical genius, Grun, whom I had sent back to Arkon about a year ago with tremendously important plans for a new weapon. Even at that time he had been of the opinion that sooner or later an inter-planar stabilization would have to take place. That is, there would have to be at least a temporarily constant overlap of the 2 time-planes. I didn't have to wait any longer for the technicians' report because I could very well imagine what they would find in the instrument records of the smaller spaceship. What Grun had expected had come into being. Precisely for this reason I had requested reinforcements.

If it was possible, from now on, for the enemy to penetrate our universe without any special technical difficulties, the whole affair could boil down to a standard battle situation. My *Tosoma* was among the older units of her class. During engagements in the Nebula Sector she had suffered more hits than a battleship really ought to have to endure and still remain in service. Inkar's battle cruiser was a newer model in the fleet. Its massive 1500-foot diameter placed it in a class with the Fusuf series. With the 2 ships I might have been able to conquer entire races of people—that is, if such people were not at a higher development than intelligence-stage G.

But now here I was with the pitiful remains of a once-proud squadron, facing an enemy whose space-flight technology was phenomenal. I was a high energy engineer and I could evaluate the significance of Lt. Kehene's observations. If alien spaceships could emerge from a paradimensional hyperspace without appreciable space-warp phenomena, this meant that their designers had mastered a considerably simpler method of trans-light travel than our own. But a lot still depended on the evaluation of the TO-4 data.

Tarth loomed before me. Not a muscle moved in his aged and furrowed features. "Any special instructions, Eminence?"

"To you, my friend, I am Atlan, the same as always,"

I told him somewhat absently. But finally I looked at my staff officers. They were all there, with a knowing gleam in their eyes.

Behind and to their left the mighty *Paito* towered on its great landing struts. It was a miracle that precisely my 2 strongest ships had remained to me from my attack squadron. There was no help to be expected from Arkon so it behooved us to act on our own in a timely manner. My veteran combat officers awaited my orders.

My gaze fell upon Kosol, the new chief of the mathematics department. Next to him I saw Capt. Feltif, our colonial planner. He had set up our 8 defense bases on Atlantis. The propulsion engines salvaged from the cruisers *Titsina* and *Volop* had been installed as stationary 5th-dimension impulse-beam projectors.

On the larger continents to the East and West of Atlantis, top specialists had erected stone fortresses, pyramid-shaped silos and other such emergency stations and billets. What we had in mind was that in case of a major attack we would evacuate the intelligent native peoples from the equatorial zone of the planet.

Aircraft were standing by in case it was necessary to also evacuate the deployed crews from their gun positions, in those areas where we might expect an interzonal meshing of the 2 time-planes. For the Arkonide settlers in Atlantis an undersea bio-survival dome had been constructed. In an emergency we could quickly house up to 10,000 people inside the dome. On the 2d planet of Larsaf's Star it had been revealed that fish and other water-based life forms were *not* entrapped by the relative-energy front, as long as they remained in the depths. This had been a valuable discovery for us.

However, all of our preparations had been made against the possibility of a normal passage of the dimension overlap. But if from here on the unknown enemy was going to be able to make a direct entry into our own continuum, the situation would take on a much darker complexion. Then it would be a matter of life & death.

I took a last look upwards at the blistered and partly melted battle scar in the side of the damaged flier. Then I turned to the waiting men. "The *Tosoma* and *Paito* are on ready alert status. Commanders will go on board. We will make an armed reconnaissance flight near the orbit of Larsa. Feltif, get your ground commandos into the gun stations and bring the impulse-cannons to idling level. Tarth, set up a hyper-com connection with the Imperator. The text of the message will be given to you shortly. Native inhabitants will be evacuated. Unfortunately families will have to be separated wherever the Arkonide married men belong to ship crews or gun crews."

I glanced at Inkar out of the corner of my eye. I had heard he was supposed to be happily married. The young commander stared straight ahead without a quiver on his face but I knew that my orders must have weighed heavily on him.

"The Arkon colonists are to be advised to make all necessary preparations for a flight into remote land areas. Henceforth our headquarters are transferred to the submarine pressure dome, which the engineering teams are to make ready for occupancy."

I looked at my watch. It was a little after mid-day. The yellow-white sun stood at its zenith above the spaceport. It was a beautiful, Arkon-kind of world with every prospect for a magnificent development. And in that moment I resolved to defend this 3d planet with every means at my disposal.

"Takeoff in 1 hour," I announced. "The instrument readouts from the TO-4 are to be brought to me at once."

I raised my hand to the men. Silently they bowed their heads. Whatever could be said at this time had been said.

Tarth, who was also Chief of Staff, walked beside me to the ground car. The old man's towering figure was a symbol of staunchness and strength. Since he had received his rejuvenation treatments his step had become livelier and more supple.

As I was about to get into the car, Tarth suddenly spoke to me. "Atlan, if it were a normal time-zone overlap we could easily avoid it because of its negligible speed. But now our only chance is to make an all-out attack and to hit them hard! If we wait around until they come at us out of that trick funnel of theirs, we are lost!"

"I know," I agreed calmly. "That's why the takeoff is set. I'm just afraid that both effects will occur at once. It's imperative that our most indispensable ships be in deep space, if there's going to be a zonal overlap at the time of opposition of the 2 planets. But right now the main thing is to see those instrument readouts from the TO-4. Let's hold everything as-is for the moment."

As we drove off we knew that we were going against our better judgment. Come what might, I was determined to make a thrust through the field-stabilization funnel in order to make one grand blasting attack of annihilation.

Before us loomed the magnificent buildings of Atlopolis, the capital city of Atlantis. It was the cultural and commercial center for our widely dispersed colonists, who had settled practically the entire continent.

Our escort vehicles cleared the way with shrill whistles. The natives, who were colorfully dressed in hand-made fabrics, sank reverently to their knees. It was always distressing to me to see people at this stage of intelligence act so submissively. However, Tarth and the colonial commandos considered a certain amount of glorification to be essential.

To my surprise I heard old Tarth grumble out an unusual suggestion: "We ought to try to train and improve the most intelligent men of this race with accelerated hypno-schooling. That's one way of finding out if they have the mental capacity at this stage to understand our technology."

I nodded with some sense of irony. My old fire-eater was gradually becoming more dove-like in his old age. Tarth had formerly counted himself among those Arkonides who landed on alien worlds and loaded their cannons before they said hello.

"Such a program has already been established," I replied.

"Huh. . .?"

I was amused by Tarth's nonplussed expression. As we sped along the broad, winding avenues toward my administrative palace, I noticed that his sharp old eyes examined the natives who were working along the verdured parkways. These tall, brown-skinned people were physically quick and strong. Whether or not their brains had developed as splendidly as their bodies would be revealed through our first experiments with the highly secret hypnotic accelerated education machines.

A thundering arose from the now distant spaceport. The thrust engines of the mighty *Tosoma* generated a fiery wreath of superheated air masses. If I had possessed 10 ships of her class I'd have felt a lot better.

40 minutes later the instrument data recorded by Lt. Kehene were transmitted to me over the video intercom system. The flagship's positronicon had worked swiftly and dependably.

Kosol, my new chief mathematician, was at the transmitter end. "It is a large-scale natural phenomenon, Eminence, which may be repeating itself about every 5 billion years. The 2 time-planes seek a mutual stabilization level, which implies a discharge of energy from the dimension having the higher state of force tension, volume-wise. Those outlet funnels are identical to unstable energy fields of much wider magnitude. They provide an assimilation of differentials in opposed field currents. Practically described, they are virtual conductors. It's conceivable that the aliens over there have grasped this fact on a mathematical basis and put it to practical use for their own purposes. The quick thrust made simultaneously by the 4 spaceships indicates that they knew the exact moment of penetration. By the same token, it seems they also can figure out when to return."

"And what are the prospects to be extrapolated from this?" I asked grimly.

"Not good for us, Your Eminence. In about 14 days a stage of complete mutual balance will be reached. What we can infer from that is that the previous state of instability will take on a stabilized condition that may be constant for weeks or even months."

There was no need for Kosol to tell me more. I thanked him and cut off the connection. Tarth stood beside the great windows of my office and brooded out at the panorama beyond. We were alone. With slow deliberation he said: "We have 2 possibilities. If we flee from here this world will be spared from a nuclear inferno but the organic life here including the people would then disappear without a trace. And that would cause an interruption of natural development. But if we put up a resistance, things will really get hot—mark my words! It's possible for #3 to be turned into a glowing oven."

He looked at me pensively as I answered him calmly:

"You took the words out of my mouth, old friend. I'll have to chance it. Even if half of this world is destroyed there will still be enough livable areas left to save the present intelligences from an ultimate doom. However, we shall attempt to repel the enemy."

Tarth said no more. His broad hand clapped loudly against the left side of his chest. His commander's radio helmet, decorated with planetary symbols, was clamped tightly under his arm as he strode stiffly toward the door.

20 minutes later he announced from the *Tosoma* that the squadron flagship was ready to go into deep space.

As I was leaving my headquarters, the *Paito* was already blasting through the brilliant blue skies over Atlantis. Below in the great harbor of the island continent, the native fishermen and merchant sailors frantically reefed in the colorful sails of their wooden ships. From sad experience they had learned how devastating the shockwaves from a large ascending spaceship could be.

At the groundlevel airlock of the *Tosoma* a fleet ceremony met me with the usual demonstration of homage. Tarth placed great value on usage and custom. 3 minutes later the impulse converters of the 15 remaining propulsion engines were cautiously extended. We took off in a torrent of sound that was like an erupting volcano.

Empty space opened before us. The 3d planet fell away and quickly became a shimmering ball of reflected light. Owing to the conversion of 3 propulsion units into hyper-dimensional energy projectors, it now required almost 13 minutes for us to reach the natural speed of light. So the old *Tosoma* was no longer the kind of ship that should be waging a modern space war. We flew a direct course toward Larsa, the 2d planet of the system. The primeval jungle world was supposed to have been stripped bare not only of all human life, according to reports, but of most of its animal life as well. Due to the numerous passages of the relative-energy front, all creatures had been dragged into the other time-plane. We were not particularly fond of the idea that Larsaf #3 should suffer a similar fate.

5/ PREPARING FOR BATTLE

Everything worked out quite differently from what I had imagined. Those energy discharge formations that mathematician Kosol had called "outlet funnels" turned out to be unpredictable in their nature. Whenever such a phenomenon occurred we never knew exactly how long it would hold.

Our ship's positronicon was one of the most modern calculation units in the Greater Empire. In spite of this it was unable to determine the definite intervals of the occurrences or even to approximate the persistence time of the discharging energy fields. We were lacking observational data obtained over a longer period, on the basis of which we might have derived more exact constants for a reference.

There wasn't a thing more that we could do with the orthodox type of 4-dimensional math. A non-linear proportional calculation of the approaching total overlap was easy enough to carry out on the program board of the machine but the results never aligned themselves with reality.

Then we tried to approach the problem with the hyper-math section of the robot brain. But that only led to such garbled results that it was senseless to even discuss them. Finally we recognized that the outlet funnels must be some kind of lightning discharge but which functioned abnormally and were subject to completely different laws.

We were not dealing with 5th dimensional field quantities but with something that was based on normal universe phenomena. The fluctuating factors could only be identified with some sort of incomprehensible time-rate shift, all of which took on an increasingly unstable configuration in the course of a mutual field stabilization.

Naturally the unknown enemy was much better acquainted with the laws of their plane of existence than we were.

After we had been merely observing in outer space for 8 days, the enemy's spaceships broke through the strange discharge field for the 2d time. At the last moment I had just about given up the idea of hostile action. We had moved far enough away so that we did not have to expose ourselves to the enemy fire.

Nevertheless we learned an important lesson from the incident!

When alien ships appeared so swiftly there was practically never any space-warp distortion, whereas with our own trans-light technique a hyper-shockwave was quite inevitable. My mathematical section had figured out that the aliens more or less flew through the 5th dimension. This was a very essential difference from the hyperjump or transition method which we used.

Secondly, the spaceships we detected never moved faster than 50% the speed of light, although our energy detectors indicated that their propulsion engines were running at full power.

Thirdly, the mysterious foe only came through when the outlet funnels held their stability for at least 3 hours!

That was probably the most important discovery of them all. It meant that the enemy knew exactly when he could depend on such energy formations and when he could not!

Within about a week, therefore, we picked up some very good data. In our own space the enemy apparently couldn't fly faster than ½ light-speed. In addition, he used a linear hyperspace flight technique and he could also calculate the life expectancy of a funnel forcefield.

Those were 3 fundamental factors on which we could build up a system of prediction. If I had had an Arkonide fleet at my disposal, the phantom would have been

eliminated in a few days. I might have risked sending a robot-piloted battleship through the first likely discharge channel. Then we would have certainly demonstrated the effectiveness of our weapons on the "other side"!

* * * *

Since our top alert takeoff, 11 days of Atlantis time had passed. I stood off at a distance of only 6 million miles from the 2d planet with my 2 fighting units. The remarkable magnifying circuits of our telescopicameras gave us a clear view through the thick cloud covering of the jungle world.

Down there hardly any organic life remained.

However the robot Brain that had been built on Larsaf 2 under my regency did not appear to have been disturbed in any way. Whenever we signaled it, its hypercom reports returned promptly to us. But its instrument test results didn't tell us anything new. The fortress stronghold that I had ordered constructed for the protection of the great robot Brain had not been activated or brought into action at any time.

"Because nobody's around anymore!" commented Tarth grimly when he heard about it.

Until now the 3d planet had been spared from any of these weird phenomena but now worlds 2 & 3 approached each other more closely from day to day. A full opposition was imminent. By now we should be feeling the influence of the time wall's advance offshoots.

I looked thoughtfully at the giant viewscreens of the panoramic gallery. The *Paito* was about 60 miles away. We could still communicate clearly by normal radio. Our flight speed amounted to only 6200 miles per second but the emergency spots at all machine controls were doubly manned.

We were waiting for the next outlet funnel to appear. My plan was set. If we were to see or track enemy ships, we would leap to the edge of the discharge field in a fast, short transition and penetrate through in a surprise forward thrust. But under no circumstance were we to remain more than 1 hour of standard time in the other continuum. Our assumption that a return would be impossible after collapse of a funnel was well-grounded. The enemy forces appeared to be subject to the same difficulty because they made a panic course change for home every time they reached a time limit.

Nostalgically I gazed at a distant, barely discernible

light-point which in reality embodied an entire star cluster. There lay Arkon, our home world. There a bitter battle of life & death was being fought for the survival of the Arkonide race and the Greater Empire.

We had not received any further messages. My hypercom dispatch had remained unanswered. I had long since given up the idea of ever getting reinforcements in either ships or repair equipment and supplies. As soon as this thing with the unknown aliens was cleared up, I intended to offer my services again as a fleet commander. Granted, of course, that I at least came out of this with 1 large spaceship. I could not risk any more losses or our return would be prohibited forever.

I was just about to discuss the detailed possibilities with Tarth when the radio officer on duty stepped into the Command Central. In his hand was a decoded foil strip.

Capt. Masal silently saluted. "More troubles, Your Eminence," he said, hesitantly. "A message from Feltif. The colonists refuse to leave their farms. They base their refusal to obey orders on the fact that they are subordinate to the civil rights legislation of a colonization board but not to a Fleet admiral. Furthermore, Feltif informs you that our settlers have taken precautions to reinforce the undermanned ground defense positions in case of an attack."

I closed my eyes and took in a deep breath. I had expected as much! The people were 2d generation Arkonides. They were descendants from the planet Zakreb 5, which had formerly been settled by true Arkonides. Their offspring had been forced to emigrate again because the colonial world had already become overpopulated.

"You mean to say they refuse to go to the undersea pressure dome?" asked Tarth in bewilderment.

"Oh yes. They have a deep aversion to the water and the confined close quarters down there."

I reached for the deciphered dispatch. The text was clear enough. In the issuance of orders I had overlooked the fact that the settlers came from a dry, poorly watered world. From the standpoint of colonial psychology it was wrong to assign them to an undersea dome as a refuge.

"Are you going to stand for that?"

I looked at Tarth with a deliberate coolness. This was a decision he would have to leave to me. "Am I supposed to use force to drive the Zakreb people under the sea? And if so—what with? With crewmen from the ships or perhaps the 300 soldiers in the ground positions?"

The commander pressed his lips together. Anger flashed in his eyes. To Tarth this insubordination was tantamount to high treason. Our acute lack of personnel seemed to be beside the point.

Due to its still inadequate automation, the old *Tosoma* required 3000 crewmen. The modern *Paito* managed with as little as 600 specialists. The remainder of my fighting men were in the Atlantis ground positions. It was foolish to think of forcing the obstinate colonists.

I turned to Capt. Masal. "Message to Feltif, Fleet code A-13-BQ, pulse transmission. The settlers are to be advised that in case of an attack an evacuation is no longer possible. In consideration of my vital responsibilities, which have recently come to include the task of protecting the entire world from annihilation, rescue assistance can no longer be guaranteed. The colonists are hereby at liberty to act at their own discretion. However, under these conditions I can no longer accept any responsibility for the results of coming events."

Minutes later, the pulse-modulated dispatch was transmitted. Its reception was confirmed by Capt. Feltif. Shortly thereafter, information was received to the effect that the Farmers' Mutual Trust Council had accepted my decision with the greatest satisfaction.

I handed the return dispatch to the First Officer of the battleship. The smile on my face must have been somewhat puzzling to the men. "File this and also have it registered in the positronic memory bank. It might come to pass that we'll be asked later to explain how 10,000 Zakreb settlers could perish."

"Peasants!" snorted Tarth with all the scorn of which he was capable. "Impertinent and presumptuous louts who can't see any farther than the nearest nuclear-powered tractor, which they also expect to be furnished by the State."

With that the case was closed for the old warhorse. I was certain that in an emergency Tarth would not lift a finger to help the settlers now. For my part, I had neither the inclination nor the time to bother with any more internal problems.

In this respect, however, the native inhabitants of Larsaf 3 were wiser in their attitude. It may perhaps have been something in their primitive instincts which caused them to regard my instructions as an unavoidable decree. Which could of course save them, perhaps all of them. I was very fond of these tall, powerful people with their velvety skins and their peaceful, unrebellious conduct. I couldn't remember having gotten along so well with an underdeveloped colonial race as I had with the Atlanteans. One day they would rise to become a great and powerful nation. It was not within my responsibilities to encroach upon their natural development but it was within my province to defend this people's homeland.

I asked the First Officer to bring me the appropriate sections of the colonial laws. According to these I was even duty-bound to guarantee the protection of the Empire to any willingly subject race of people.

In the midst of this train of thought I also made a decision that I would go by the book and make the enemy officially and fully aware of my intentions.

Masal appeared in the giant Command Central. I dictated to him the Declaration of War according to Article 16, Volume 2, of the Emergency Powers Code for all commanding officers of the Fleet who were operating outside the boundaries of the Empire.

I had the open broadcast sent out at repeated intervals of 10 minutes. When the next outlet funnel appeared at a distance of only 3,000,000 I had the *Tosoma's* beam transmitter send the same message right into the gaping throat of the discharge zone. There was nothing more I could do. Besides, the attack on Kehene's auxiliary craft was unquestionably to be regarded as an act of war.

The discharge field disappeared within only 14 minutes. The phenomenon was one of those unstable or short-time quantities whose duration we could not calculate in spite of ourselves.

I looked at my watch and wondered whether or not I should lift the full battle alert status for an hour or so. My men were strained to the breaking point and in some cases exhausted. Then something happened for which I was not prepared. A 2d discharge funnel became visible just about 5 minutes after the first one had disappeared. In spite of the latent danger involved, I was fascinated. The image took form in what appeared to be empty space and yet I knew the end of one continuum was there where the other universe was overlapping into ours.

The funnel was long and narrow; at least so it seemed. Our instantly operating instruments revealed that its maximum diameter was nevertheless about 3.6 million miles. It became ever more visible as it continued to load up with the energy charge from the other plane. Owing to its deep reddish glow the funnel mouth loomed up clearly against the darkness of interstellar space. Somehow it seemed to be composed of solid material, since it blotted out the distant stars and either absorbed or reflected their light.

The opening was turned toward us at an angle of 43.7 °.

Silently we watched the darkish opening with its mottled bright red background. Seconds later the alarm whistles began to shrill, jolting me to new alertness.

The matter detectors were in sync with the screens of the main tracking center and now they were showing us 7 green-shimmering points of light. At the same time a fluorescent diagrammatic curve gave us information concerning the material composition of the observed objects.

10 seconds later we knew that we were dealing with the attackers' spaceships. Another 10 seconds after that our reconnaissance flight speed was increased by the full thrust of the engines.

I switched on a full alarm. When the sirens began to howl, the 3000 men on board the *Tosoma* knew that the long-promised attack they had been drilling for so ceaselessly had at last arrived. If the aliens were sending 7 ships this time into our space all at once, it was a guaranteed certainty that the discharge funnel was stable.

From that point on we were on automatic controls. I listened to the roar of the engines, observed the flickering control lamps of the weapons circuits and checked the power meters of the fully loaded inertial absorbers, which were protecting us from the g effects of high acceleration.

Since we were short 3 propulsion units I ordered that the remaining 15 units be held to maximum emergency output. The tanks for the nuclear fuel additive had been filled in Atlantis. We had made use of bismuth, which was abundant on Larsaf 3. So in spite of the low flight acceleration rate of 300 mps^2 we began to get into the border areas of relativistic velocity.

The outer edge of the funnel was about 12,000,000 miles distant. 11 minutes and 3 seconds after our first sighting the coordinate data of the lightning swift hyper-transition computer were at hand, thus making us ready for a short jump. I activated the transition impulse control as we were finally picked up by the tracking beams of the alien ships. We registered the impact of their hyper-transmissions, which would return to their receivers as an echo.

Obviously the enemy used another, very inadequate tracking method or some relativistic-physical effect was present which caused a shift of time-rate. At any rate our own detection of them had happened immediately. The aliens were just now becoming aware that 2 heavy class fighting ships were in their immediate vicinity and that their defensive and offensive weapons were by no means to be compared to those of the small auxiliary flier.

". . .and we thank the Imperator for what he has bestowed upon us!"

I had caught the final words of the battle ritual, spoken by Tarth. In the Fleet it was an ancient tradition for the commander to call out these words through the communicators, shortly before the battle. This required a solemn and high-sounding delivery. An element would have been missing from the moment if Tarth had remained silent.

When the hypertrans computer time-released the transition impulse I had sent it, we had reached 82% the speed of light. Owing to her higher acceleration, the *Paito* kept a formation distance of 12,000 miles from us.

Then followed the brief pain of dematerialization as we went into transition. We hardly noticed the accompanying phenomena but I could still hear the strange moaning sound of the space-warp generator. Then my senses dimmed.

6/ ARKON DOES NOT ANSWER

My Commander's chair was shaking violently. It lasted only a few moments until I had regained my senses. A contact release turned off the automatic vibrator equipment.

In the *Tosoma's* Command Central a hundred heavy thunderstorms seemed to have broken out all at once. The weapons forming the "green" broadside fired in a breathtakingly swift, concerted rhythm. Naturally this was the integrated fire control positronic, which had picked up the targets much faster than we could have and was firing at volley tempo.

When my vision cleared I saw that we had jumped right into the thick of it. The 7 enemy units had been taken completely by surprise.

Before I could even give my instructions over the microphone, the U-battery of "green" side had already opened up with effective fire. Because of the airlessness of space I could not actually see the yard-wide beams of solar-magnitude heat energy going out but I was well able to hear the signal bells from the trans-light-speed energy tracker, which announced a heavy explosion in the immediate vicinity. Seconds later the light reached us.

On the panoramic viewscreens, 2 nuclear sunballs blossomed simultaneously. 2 light-points became hand-sized balls of livid heat, which then expanded into mammoth, blue-white spheres of incandescent fire.

"Target 1 out, target 4 out—destruction total," came the automatic tinny-voiced announcement from the fire control robot.

The indicator board's flickering lights told me that the gun turrets had swung about. We were firing with everything we had on board. Under the molecular-decohesion effect of the disintegrator guns, another enemy ship blew into a fluorescent cloud of atomized vapor. On the sweep radar screens, of course, this phenomenon was only discernible as a sort of electronic bas relief.

In spite of everything happening so fast that it was almost beyond the human threshold of comprehension and response, Tarth had to switch to manual control because what was coming up was not programmable. We were racing directly through the enemy formation and before us gaped the maw of the funnel. There was no more time for the running battle, since our course was opposed to that of the enemy ships and the moment of effective range became negligible.

I noticed 2 other explosions which had apparently been generated by the *Paito*, following close on our heels. Thus in one single blitz attack the enemy had lost 5 ships out of a total of 7.

It became clear to me that the unknown foe was immeasurably outclassed by Arkonide battle experience. Naturally they would have to learn this fact, and more or less swiftly, as had been the case with all of our other enemies—except for the Methans.

The hit-counter babbled at us but the muffled detonation was almost drowned out by the thunder of our engines driving at full power. The indicators revealed that our 3-ply defense screen had been hit by a thermobeam. The impact was markedly small, almost pitiable. With such weapons there could be no chance against a major battleship of the *Tosoma's* class.

Tarth roared with laughter. "Ho-ho! Their defense screens are miserable and their attack weapons are even more of a disgrace! I—"

A frightful howling sound drowned out his words. We had shot down into what Kosol called a discharge field. Our magneto-hyper-grav defense screen began to show a sphere of flames around our hull, which could be seen in the optical viewscreens. This meant that we were penetrating some sort of finely attenuated matter.

The howling sharpened to a sustained screaming as we neared the narrow end of the funnel. The individual power plants of the *Tosoma* were running at their highest capacity. The automatic power controls shut down all peripheral equipment operations that were not absolutely vital.

All I could still see in the viewscreens was a writhing, flaming field of red. It was an unheard of gamble to thrust forward into this uncanny pattern of forces at almost the speed of light. For some time now there had been nothing to indicate the presence of the remaining 2 enemy ships. They were probably going through a wild braking maneuver by now. Their commanders must still be feeling the chill of terror in their bones—that is, if they actually had any bones or limbs at all!

Reports from the different ship sections were avalanching. Tarth sat close beside me in his commander chair, his lips moving without my being able to understand a word. The howling screams of our passage continued blasting our ears. Titanic explosions of force racked our protective screens, shaking the *Tosoma's* hull in every joint and seam.

The auto-controls of our spacesuits clapped our helmets over our heads and covered our ears with cushioned noise dampeners, at the same time turning on our suit communication systems.

I was just thinking that I had taken too great a risk in plunging thus precipitately into this unknown nothingness, when suddenly the storm of raging forces ceased.

The sea of flames covering the defense screens disappeared almost simultaneously and before us in empty space we saw a great, deep-red sun.

It was as if we had popped out of a transition and entered an alien solar system but the impression was deceiving. Instantly I missed the deep blackness of our own universe. Here everything appeared to be shrouded in a sort of dark red twilight haze. The constellations were entirely alien and in this time-plane our light-speed flight took on the aspect of something monstrous and frighteningly unreal. We were hurtling toward the red sun faster than we actually should be.

I heard Tarth giving out orders. It was his responsibility to bring the ship out of the danger zone as fast as possible. Our matter detectors showed 3 planets at a fairly close distance from us. The coordinate readouts were produced more swiftly than even our excellent positronicomputer had ever been able to before. The roaring of our engines increased beyond measurement. I knew that Tarth had thrown in the last reserves. We made our escape maneuver using the plasma afterburners, which added another 80,000 pounds of thrust.

Behind us the hurtling *Paito* held easily to our course, also driving out of the danger area at emergency full thrust. As we passed the giant red star, our widely-extended outer screens were again besieged by ravening forces. Then we were through and beyond it.

Our hypercom connection with the *Paito* happened so abruptly that I suddenly realized the theory of alternate time-planes was demonstrating itself. As a result of our daring maneuver, what we had brought along with us was something that could only be called a relativistic quantity: namely, our own stable time reference.

Based on the empirical evidence of our observations, what was happening was that we were moving twice as fast as any equivalent time-rated event in this universe.

Far ahead of us appeared a planet that also glimmered with the same reddish light. Our flight was so swift that it seemed we were suddenly going 1000 times faster than light. So the time had come for action. The analytical instrumentation buzzed and hummed. The world ahead had a thick atmosphere, classed as an oxygen type. By a strange coincidence it was also Planet 3 of this particular system. It was as though it were a parallel to our own frame of reference back in the system we had come from.

Once again I sent out the official declaration of war on the hyperbeam. Then we swept past the 2d planet so closely that we were forced to make an evasive curve around it.

The *Paito*, commanded by Capt. Inkar, now came into closer formation with us. I could see him clearly on the regular TV hookup. Tarth gazed at me searchingly. His lips were compressed and his jaw was set in his hard-lined face.

I switched to general fleet com and picked up the microphone. "Squadron leader to all hands: the energy readouts on Planet 3 ahead show that spaceship bases, major-class power plants and energy-beam projector installations have to be present. What we have to assume is that this world represents a carefully developed main base, so positioned that the enemy can launch an attack every time he figures out when a discharge field is going to form. We will attack in accordance with the Nebula Sector Plan, using all available weapons. We will make a double target pass, the *Paito* on polar course, the *Tosoma* taking north and south belts of the equatorial line. Following the attack run, we assemble at our entry point and fly non-formation back through the funnel. Neither ship waits for the other one. Once in normal space, suspend space battle operations and fly directly to Larsaf 3, where you will prepare to make a defensive stand against any enemy units that might break through. You will operate on the assumption that there *will* be pursuit. That is all—confirm!"

All commanders had understood. There were no further questions. The Nebula Sector Plan covered all contingencies in the type of blitz attack we were contemplating and which we had carried out on many other occasions. At best, of course, the plan was based largely on our experiences with the methane breathers. It had not yet been applied to an unknown enemy who could easily depopulate entire planets and blast a reconnaissance ship without any warning.

Neither in the legislation nor mental makeup of my venerable race was there any provision or inclination to hesitate or hold back in such a case as this. Our 5000 years of galactic politics had led us to believe that attack was the best form of defense. I was determined to either be master of the present dangerous situation or at least to show the aliens our teeth.

3 minutes later we switched to retro-thrust, braking our forward motion. It had been impossible to get any direct bearings on specific targets.

As Fleet Commander, I was provided with numerous internal surveillance devices which were designed to supply me with direct, personal information concerning the crew activity—all operating without intervention by the various section leaders. So I was able to see and hear my weapons fire control officer, Eseka, as he extended the grav-launcher in preparation for using our most dangerous attack weapon. Arkon bombs were carried to their targets by self-guided missiles capable of the speed of light. Their high-energy firing velocity was in the neighborhood of 6200 miles per second.

The warheads had the characteristic of generating an inextinguishable atomic holocaust which affected all elements having an atomic number higher than 10. We ourselves knew of no method to stop such a fire, once ignited.

I did not dare to employ the newly developed gravitation bombs in this unstable-seeming universe, since the "GRBs" were normally considered to be 5th dimensional energy weapons.

As we drew near to the planet on our prescribed course, we detected more than 100 fair-sized ships that were quite obviously preparing to make an emergency thrust out into space.

Once more I picked up the general fleet com mike. "Squadron leader to all hands: Enemy units commencing intercept maneuvers. Disregard them and prepare for atmospheric entry. Concentrate all available energy into the forward collision screens for air-molecular repulsion. Sustained attack fire, robot-controlled, fan-out attenuation within saturation factor of 5 kilotons TNT per square mile. Ready. . .? Then let them have it!"

In such operations we did not indulge in very much conversation. My men were too well coordinated with one another to require long-winded explanations.

The *Paito* disappeared beyond the planet's rim. With the giant flagship we plowed through a barely noticeable formation of enemy spaceships, followed by a rising howl of violently compressed air masses as we made our entry dive, even though we were keeping to the highest strata of the atmosphere. From the computer room came the announcement that our fairly negligible speed was nevertheless double the theoretical top velocity permissible in this time-plane.

The effects related to this development were momentarily of no concern to me. In spite of the thick ear-protectors I was wearing, my auditory senses were racked with pain. The spherical hull of the *Tosoma* resounded like a giant bell. Then on top of it the automatic weapons opened their rapid intermittent fire. By comparing our intrinsic velocity with target distances, the master positronic system was able to control the firing intervals so that a swiftly erected learning curve of empirical data resulted in a precise coalescing of range-effective areas, making an even blanket coverage.

We could not observe entirely what was going on down below. We had our hands full trying to hold the ship in its attack orbit because with our engines at full power we were exceeding the free fall limits and the resulting centrifugal force was naturally trying to hurl us on a straight line out into space.

Tarth was shopping for spare energy to throw into the forward collision shielding, even diverting the idle power from the gun turrets that were on the leeside of the firing. Our bow side entry screens were flaming white hot from atmospheric friction in spite of our passage through the thinnest upper strata.

We circled the planet in just 5½ minutes. The course-holding maneuvers were dangerous. Our overstrained equipment couldn't take the load for very long.

When we reached our starting point after the first orbital run, veering 10° north in the process, I noted on the groundward viewscreens that there was nothing but incandescent land areas and gigantic atomic mushroom clouds to be seen—the latter no doubt having been generated by fissionable or fusionable material. Probably the atomic blasts might even represent explosions of the long, cylindrical enemy ships as they were caught in our fire.

After the 2d tactical target run, the *Tosoma* peeled off and away. Maj Eseka had launched a total of 10 Arkon bombs, all of which had struck their designated target areas and ignited.

Finally the terrible thunder of the impulse and disintegrator weapons ceased abruptly. Which only enabled us to distinguish the almost equal raging and roaring of the engines and the power reactors. The battleship's mighty shell still resonated noisily with them. We still could not risk taking off our noise mufflers.

"Where is the *Paito?*" I shouted excitedly into the head mike of my helmet.

Capt. Masal responded from the tracking center: "Just coming up over the northern pole, Your Eminence. Still maintaining remote fire, accelerating, now using thermo-cannons vertically on red sector, needlepoint pattern. Apparently no enemy units visible. Now the firing has stopped—only quanta output from propulsion detectable. According to emission readings, no damages apparent. Over & out!"

I breathed a sigh of relief and turned to look at Tarth. My flagship commander smiled back at me. I heard his deep voice in my earphones:

"They won't try stealing off harmless settlers again and they'll lay off shooting up our patrol ships! By Arkon!—who are we dealing with anyway? Are they phantoms, robots or what? How is it they make use of a natural phenomenon for their dirty work? Even if you won't permit it, I'm going to make a forced flight in the *Tosoma* to Arkon and get hold of an attack fleet. I'll do it one way or another!"

"If it were not for the Methans, yes," I answered wearily, inwardly assailed by self-reproach. Had I proceeded justly? Who *were* the unknown aliens?

The throat of the outlet funnel loomed before us. We plunged into its depths at light-speed but this time to our great astonishment the previously observed effects did not occur. I was merely expecting that our forward motion would be restricted by invisible forces but this time it seemed that we were pushing through a soft, yielding mass.

The announcement was not long in coming from the power and engine control center. "Speed dropping at 75 mps in spite of full thrust, rate constant. Question: should we inject more nuclear fuel?"

I ordered it immediately, knowing full well the overload I was putting on the equipment. Behind us hurtled the battle cruiser *Paito* but Inkar had not yet hailed us.

Eternities seemed to pass before we were finally released from the funnel. Just as I was about to turn again to Tarth with a sigh of relief a report arrived from the tracking room:

"Discharge field has disappeared. No further energy variations detectable."

This calmly delivered news made me turn pale. Tarth's eyes were suddenly like saucers. Kosol's face gleamed white from the intercom screen. I saw him look hastily at his watch.

"By our own time frame we were over there just 65 minutes," he said in a troubled tone.

By *our* time-frame!" The thought almost exploded in my brain.

How could the field have vanished again? We knew that it would have to have remained stable for at least 3 hours. Had we experienced one of those feared lapse-rate changes—a reference-oriented time shift? By others' reference points did our 65 minutes equal 65 days, or even as many weeks?

I clambered slowly out of my high-backed chair and lifted the microphone with a trembling hand. "Masal, put in a call to Atlantis, quickly! Call Feltif. I have to know what may have. . ."

I didn't have to say any more. The emergency call came in under Fleet Format KRA-Q-Z. It was an automatic taped message on open channel and uncoded:

"Capt. Feltif to Squadron Chief. We are lost. 5 gun positions have been destroyed and on top of it we're faced with a very heavy overlap front. Half the colonists have been drawn into it. We are retreating with the natives into the forest wilderness and mountains. Approximately 100 enemy ships are maintaining a running attack. The axial stability of the planet is wavering. It appears that the time front has brought strong gravitational fields with it which are changing the inclination of Larsaf 3's axis to the ecliptic. This is Capt. Feltif. Where are you? I've been calling for 9 days. Arkon does not answer. End of message. Will repeat in 3 minutes, will repeat in 3 minutes."

Everybody heard the distress call. I stood there as though liquid air had been poured over me. Tarth's face was like a stone statue.

"Attack immediately, come what may," I heard myself saying.

100 ADVENTURES FROM NOW
You'll experience adventure in the
Star Jungle

7/ ATLANTIS—DYING

We gambled on a short transition jump but as we emerged out of hyperspace we found ourselves in the center of a mass formation of about 150 heavy class enemy fighter ships. None of them matched the size of the *Tosoma* and only 2 were identified as being capable of facing up to the heavy cruiser *Paito*. Nevertheless, from the first moment of battle our resistance seemed doomed to failure. We never recovered. After the first penetrating hits the defense screens of the *Paito* failed. It was structurally characteristic of heavy cruiser types that although they were fast and heavily armed the space demands of equipment installations were satisfied at the cost of defensive screening. The prescribed structural weight, by Arkon standards, could not be exceeded, and if the spherical compartments were stuffed chockful with every possible type of equipment and machinery there was simply nothing more that would go into the ship.

The proud *Paito* under Capt. Inkar was caught in a hail of fire from approximately 60 enemy ships and was detonated. The resultant energy release was equivalent to that of a miniature sun. I knew that the engine and reactor cores had gone into a chain reaction. About 50 billion tons of TNT were released, in effect.

The catastrophe occurred close to the lunar orbit. As hot as the sun, the gaseous sphere spread out so quickly that it even grazed the upper air strata of the 3d planet.

I hovered over the night hemisphere of our colonial world. The almost ultra-violet energy ball arched upward in all its splendor and might above the dark planetary horizon and turned the night into glaring day.

Even at our distance our protective screens raged with titanic forces to resist the impact. I was certain that Inkar's fiery demise had taken at least 70 enemy ships to their doom. The aliens were not yet aware of the effects of detonating a large Arkonide fighting ship.

But they learned quickly!

The *Tosoma* was still lying under a crossfire from about 80 enemy ships but suddenly the fire was lifted. The others had had a bitter lesson. They retreated frantically and did not reopen their effective fire until they were at a distance of almost 2 million miles.

They had practiced their gunnery well, these mysterious ones from another time plane. My evasive maneuvers were rash and wild. I had overridden the automatic controls in favor of manual piloting so as to move the heavy ship out of the intercepting energy beams.

It was futile! Only 5 minutes after our first enemy contact, 3 thermal shots had broken through our overloaded defense screens. A fire had broken out in power room 4. Six of our available 15 propulsion units went out. From there on the *Tosoma's* hull plates bore the brunt of everything that was being thrown at us.

Now we were close to the end. Our movements had become sluggish and more easy to calculate. We had dropped our excessive speed because even Arkonides cannot shoot perfectly if their ship is traveling near the speed of light.

The enemy had retained their rate of motion. We no longer held any special advantage over them. Per the status report the nuclear hurricane of fire from the *Tosoma's* gun turrets had annihilated 34 of the alien ships. But there were still enough of them left to polish us off.

By this time the heavily battered *Tosoma* was ablaze in 4 major sections and was falling toward the surface of the planet. Just prior to our short transition jump I had issued an order for all hands to exchange their Arkonide combat uniforms for regular spacesuits. With these very excellent apparatuses one was capable of flight and a light repulsion field for defense purposes could also be generated.

The individual protection screens were now urgently needed. The high-pitched hissing sound of the flagship's automatic fire-fighting equipment had already ceased because of breakdown. As a result, the countless safety hatches had long since closed. The individual compartments—and there were hundreds of them—had all been hermetically sealed.

The only method of combating the fire now was to withdraw the synthetic atmosphere from the interior. Without oxygen there could be no process of molecular combustion. I had no sooner gotten such a program underway than the air-pumping system broke down. Of course the positronicon sounded an alarm but that didn't serve much purpose anymore.

The fire continued unabated in the engine and power rooms. If the highly volatile fuel catalyst were to be ignited, the enemy would experience an even greater explosion. For the time being, however, the special tanks held up, since they could withstand temperatures up to 50,000 °.

About 60% of the videophone connections were knocked out, as well, so all I had left was the radio intercom system.

As the long, cylindrical ships of the enemy opened their pincers formation in order to get to a safe distance from us, we were temporarily in the lee of their fire. The aliens had stern-mounted propulsion engines whose thrust impulses apparently interfered with the automatic target tracking. At least we suddenly found ourselves free of their fire barrage. I used the opportunity to drop the *Tosoma* toward the 3d planet's nearby air envelope. As we made entry, a whistling and howling arose outside. Our usually dependable collision shields had by this time become very weak so that they could hardly ionize the air molecules. And without electrostatic charging, no electromagnetic repulsion could be effected.

Thus it developed that my flagship soon raced through the thin upper strata looking like a red-glowing sunball. In spite of this I maintained a respectable rate of descent. Our Arkonide armorplate hull could withstand 50,000 ° and the air-conditioning system was still operating.

It was clear to me that we were out of the fighting, without a chance. So I did what any responsible commander-in-chief would have done in such a situation. I was not of the maudlin, romantic school who fancied plunging heroically to a flaming death. What everything depended on now was the possibility of saving the crew survivors so that later we could put in a call for help from the home planet.

"The course is set," announced the First Officer. "Atlantis is ahead in the daylight zone."

I was planning to land the battered *Tosoma* near Atlopolis and set up a temporary ground defense, to provide fire cover so that the men could escape into the undersea dome.

We were flying at about a 60-mile altitude over the eastern continent which was heavily covered with jungles and populated by extremely primitive dark-skinned savages. Shortly thereafter the broad expanse of the ocean came into view and finally the coastal mountains of Atlantis.

* * * *

I heard a muttered curse from Tarth. Above the approaching land rose flaming mushroom clouds. The enemy seemed to have known exactly where the only defense installations were to be found on this world. Moments later we heard from the tracking and detection center. 5 spaceships had landed near the coast. Apparently troops were disembarking.

"We aren't picking up any cellular vibrations," announced Capt. Masal from the still-undamaged Com Central. "They are robots."

My orders went out to the weapons officers. The mighty *Tosoma* prepared to show its claws for the last time.

Tarth spoke with deadly calm over the helmet radio com. "Do you think their noses would be up in the air very long if *my* ship were crippled?"

Further communication was drowned out by the terrible thunder of a broadside volley. The 5 enemy ships on the land went up in a tornado of explosions and glowing flames.

I groaned aloud when the capital city and the harbor appeared on the viewscreens. The entire terrain was a single crater. All that was left of the buildings of Atlopolis were a few smoking ruins. Mile-wide thermal impact patterns had seared the countryside. There where we had installed our stationary impulse weapons, dark mushroom clouds towered over the landscape. Capt. Feltif did not answer. Our calls were not even met with an answering echo. I realized then that my ground commandos did not exist anymore. What had happened to the settlers I could well imagine.

In deep space another overlap front was forming again. We noticed it because of a strange discoloration of the stars and a shimmering in the atmosphere. And now the enemy added his renewed attacks to the forces of nature.

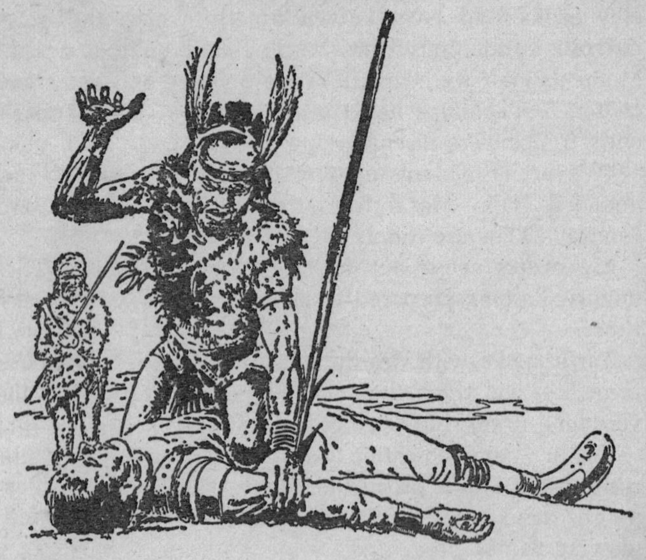

The *Tosoma* was barely capable of flight by now and Tarth flew it totally on manual controls. The auto-pilot facilities had ceased to function and all command links to engine and power room control centers had gone out of commission. The temperature rose in the Command Central, indicating that terrible fires must be raging around us.

I carried out what I had planned to do. It was imperative at all costs to keep the battleship airborne as long as possible so that it could provide a protective cover until the robot-controlled entrance locks of the undersea dome had been opened.

For security reasons a control had been set up that was based on a few individual vibratory identities. There were only 3 Arkonides that the gates would open for. Any visitors not thus recognized by the dome's robot brain would not only be left swimming helplessly before the great steel portals; they would be shot by the powerful weapons of the fortress.

The men who were authorized to enter were Capt. Feltif, chief of ground forces and the person responsible for evacuation measures—now missing; the new chief mathematician, Kosol, who was located on board my flagship; and I was the 3d person whose individual vibrations would be recognized by the robot crew.

I had to see to it as quickly as possible now that Kosol got underway. He had to use one of the pressure-screened undersea vehicles to get down below and open the gates so that the entry would be clear for us. While he was busy with that, I was to run a defense with the *Tosoma* against any possible interference attacks and prepare to make a blitz landing when I could get the men to safety. We assumed that the enemy had not detected the presence of the undersea dome, since the surface gun positions had offered much more obvious targets.

I brought our coasting speed to a stop and brought the still usable antigrav fields into play. The battleship hovered in the air above the razed harbor area. The helmet radio of my combat spacesuit worked flawlessly in response to a hand button control.

"Atlan to chief mathematician Kosol. Project Salvage now in effect. Leave your station, land in your flying spacesuit and proceed to open the locks of the pressure dome. Kosol, calling Kosol, please answer!"

Within a second or so the answer returned. The face

of a young officer appeared on the mini-screen inside my helmet, on a level just above my eyes.

"Lt. Einkal, Eminence, fire-fighting post 18. Chief mathematician Kosol is dead; the computer section is burning—all bulkhead hatches sealed off. The adjacent compartments are also on fire. Fresh air keeps coming in through large rents in the hull. Over & out!"

I heard my own involuntary outcry over this news. Close beside me, Tarth swung around in his commander seat. He had understood more swiftly than I.

"Out of here, Admiral!" he shouted at me. "Out! Get out as fast as you can! I'll handle the coverage of the retreat. Go down there, open the dome and then give me the landing instructions over the helmet radio com. Get going—what are you waiting for?"

"I—I will not leave my flagship prior to my crew!" I said harshly.

Tarth laughed humorlessly. He was incredibly cool and collected. "I'll have to throw you out. You're obligated by duty to save your men, above all. I don't need you to skipper the ship since no more tactical decisions are involved. Open the dome, Atlan! Kosol is dead and Feltif is missing. In ½ hour the time-front will be here and all life will disappear into the other plane. Don't worry about the enemy ships—I can take care of those spacegoing sewer pipes. You know I'm no greenhorn when it comes to atmospheric in-fighting. Now you get going!"

He fairly bellowed these last words. 2 heavy fighter robots trudged over toward me under remote command of Lt. Cunor. I was torn from my seat and carried bodily to the Command Central's escape tube. Tarth responded to my transport of rage with ringing laughter.

"We'll be waiting for your radio signal—'Atlan' 3

times, by word or code, and I'll risk the landing. Until that time I have a few things still left to do. Go, my friend, and bear in mind that I honor you and your family."

Before me the round lid of the emergency exit opened —a 3-foot tube that ran a straight 1200 feet to end in a fully-automated air chamber. Using this piece of equipment the crew of the Command Central could exit swiftly from the midship area.

As they closed the lid on me I was still yelling in a frenzy of rage. The stream of compressed air converted my body into a projectile. These crash exit tubes were not especially comfortable but were commensurately practical. I landed in a bed of compressed air inside the reception chamber, hard put to land on my feet. Instantly I dodged aside as another body came shooting through. It was Lt. Cunor whose robots had made short work of dumping me into the tube.

"I'll bring you before a ship's court martial!" I shouted, beside myself, and grasped him by the shoulders.

Naturally I wasn't able to carry out my threat any further because the heavy armorplate hatches glided upward and we were swirled outward into the open by a second jolt of compressed air.

I pressed a button switch that activated my flying equipment. In the spacesuit's backpak the combined micro-reactor and mini-powerpak were already humming away. The antigrav auto-control stabilized my flight so that all I had left to do was make sure that my small pulse-engine started. Behind me was Lt. Cunor, one of the most audacious and daring officers of the flagship. And of course he had been ordered by Tarth to accompany me on my difficult way.

"Lots of luck!" Tarth's voice rattled in my ears as I

saw his face on the tiny screen inside my helmet. "Can I blast out now? We're picking up new images on the trackers."

"You're not off the hook yet," I told him, although by this time my anger had subsided somewhat. "That was a blatant violation of orders involving physical constraint as well. So you'd better prepare yourself, Old Man!"

He only laughed and in the end it was all we could do to get out of the suction of the giant ship as it started off again. At a safe distance, Tarth picked up speed. Spewing flames, the *Tosoma* hurtled into a sky darkened by nuclear clouds. When it disappeared and the deep rumbling of air masses crashing into the vacuum of its wake subsided, I heard Cunor speaking warily.

"There's a high gamma fallout, Eminence. Our friends must be using old-fashioned bombs."

He had no sooner spoken than a new rumbling was heard. A gleaming phantom shot past far overhead but simultaneously opened up with its guns. I was hurled from my course by a hard shockwave and then a storm of fire raged over the tortured land. My palatial government seat had been annihilated. All I could see of it were the still-smoking remains. Far & wide there was not a sign of any living creature. It became clear to me that the transit of the relative time-zone that Feltif had reported had resulted in sucking up everything that even remotely resembled an organism. Only vegetation had remained but that had been destroyed by the unleashed storm of atomic forces.

We drifted along close above the fire-scarred ground, circumnavigated the ruins of Atlopolis and turned our flight toward the open sea.

It was then I noticed that the ocean seemed to be

stirred up by a typhoon—that is, such was my impression for about a second! After the shockwave from the attacking ship subsided, the air itself was fairly calm. In spite of this the raging waters towered into foaming breakers. The peninsula that had protected the harbor was nowhere to be seen. Farther to the East the ocean inundated the shorelines and swallowed up great stretches of land.

To the West of our location the ground had cracked open. The old volcanoes which we had considered long extinct had opened their craters to spill forth death and destruction. The thundering and rumbling was not being caused by a battle but by the forces of Nature.

"Atlantis is sinking!" shouted Cunor, horrified.

It was then that I perceived clearly that the ground was swaying. It was the most tremendous earthquake I had ever witnessed. In the distance a typhoon was brewing, the first gusts already howling across the sinking island.

The inner harbor basin was already flooded over. The breakers came onward as though intending to swallow all of Atlantis in a matter of minutes.

We landed close beside the boat bunkers that had been carved out of the high rocky headlands with disintegrators but the land was still sinking. Even as I opened the bunker doors the water was washing about my feet. Normally we would have had to take the pressure-screened vehicles 100 feet below to reach sea level.

Cunor prepared one of the special machines for operation. It was a craft built for the Fleet, which was intended for use in land operations on impassable water planets or swamp-covered worlds.

Meanwhile I attempted to get in touch with the *Tosoma.* I succeeded on the first try. The highly sensitive special equipment on the flagship could still receive the weak signals from my helmet transmitter and amplify them in their receiver a million times.

"Everything alright on board." In my helmet loudspeaker, Tarth's answer was garbled by interference sounds. "I'm just weaving in & out of their fire and taking occasional potshots. How far along are you?"

"We're just getting on board. Be careful—the island appears to be going down. We've registered powerful earthquakes."

"The whole planet's acting crazy. In the big ocean to the West, a new continent is rising out of the waters. The axial position of this world is changing! We can expect to see a global deluge! Over & out!"

As I closed the pressure-resistant cupola of the flat glider we were washed out of the bunker by the frothing waves. For some moments the craft danced about in the quake-shaken turbulent water, while Cunor pointed eastward silently.

I suppressed a cry of horror when I saw the titanic moving front of overlapping time-zones. It must have had a velocity of more than 6000 miles per hour. Its presence was discernible because of the shimmering of the air and the darkening of the sunlight as it progressed. It occurred to me then that we had lost 9 days because of a mysterious time shift—and meanwhile the dreaded full opposition of Planets 2 & 3 had arrived.

The swiftly traveling catastrophe approached us silently. It was a typical overlap curtain that spared no form of life in its wide sweep.

Cunor swung down the rheostat lever of the gravomechanical pressure screen. Immediately the water was pressed back away from the boat hull. An air-exhausted zone was generated which acted as a protective cushion between the thin hull material and the pressing water.

The flood tanks filled. We sank like a stone. We didn't notice a lessening turbulence until we had descended 150 feet beneath the surface. However such powerful submarine shockwaves assailed us that I feared for the stability of our screen.

The infra-red searchlights snapped on. We looked for the pressure dome that Feltif's specialists had constructed, knowing it must be about 50 fathoms under the surface. I had only been there once before for the purpose of having the impulse detector of the guiding robot brain pick up my physical vibrations.

I knew that at this depth a submarine plateau began, its massive cliffs reaching to the ocean floor. We had anchored the foundation of the structure there. The dome could withstand any conceivable pressure because in an emergency it could be strengthened by repulsion screens.

But the plateau could not be found! Cunor's face paled so swiftly that I could clearly guess his thoughts. The ground quakes had also swept our last refuge place into the deeps.

"Down!" I ordered harshly. "Down deeper! The dome can't have been destroyed. Its anchorage pilings were built into the planet with Arkon steel using thermal injection-molding. I'd like to see any force of Nature capable of loosening it!"

Cunor nodded resignedly. At the same time I thought despairingly of the men on the *Tosoma* who by this time must be in a frightful predicament. I dispensed with the last of my inner resistance and called to the dome's robot station over the submarine transmitter. The control machine answered immediately.

We were gripped by remote guidance controls and drawn downward at a dizzying pace. The 400-foot diameter stronghold was ground-fastened but the ground kept sinking. By the time we could finally make out the bluish gleaming contours of the dome we were more than 550 fathoms deep.

The identification surveillance by the robot brain was accomplished by means of the prescribed brain-frequency test. I placed the feedback probes on my skull and turned on the transmitter.

"Entrance permitted, Your Eminence," came the tinny voice of the automaton a few seconds later.

We were taken hold of by a tractor beam and hauled with breathtaking speed into the opening high-pressure lock. I listened impatiently to the high-pitched whining of the pumps. When the chamber was empty and air streamed in, I instructed Cunor hastily: "Wait here. I'll put in the program add-word that will make the gates respond to normal code signals. Then we have to go up again in order to call the *Tosoma.* It's no longer possible to call them from this depth. The dome doesn't have a hyper-transmitter."

A plastic-covered robot simulating an Arkonide appeared in the inner lock port. I simply dashed by him and sprang up the few spiral stairs to the programming room.

Beyond the dome was heard a rumbling and thundering. The laboring sounds of the mighty energy station indicated to me that the central brain was compensating for the resulting pressures with protective force screens. There was an alarming grinding and crunching sound in the foundation. The pressure effects of the stone masses moved by the quake must have been of unimaginable magnitude.

A violent movement suddenly flung me to the deck. I waited until the wave of earth termors had passed and then staggered, gasping, into the control room. The CPU or Central Programming Unit of the small but highly effective brain was incased in a man-high, bell-shaped steel cabinet. I was received with a stereotyped "Welcome, Your Eminence."

Wordlessly I ran my fingers over the program board in order to cancel the individual block mode of the machine's operation, placing it instead in the normal mode where it would open the locks to ordinary code signals. The call word was identical to my name.

Without questioning the machine, I ran back to the main lock. Cunor was waiting impatiently. "Over a mile deep already," he announced with amazing composure.

I paid no heed to it. Moments later we were out in the water again but this time a number of erupting volcanoes here & there on the seabottom turned the waters into dangerous, steel-hard looking spouts—submarine pillars of turbulence that glowed red from the flaming undersea eruptions.

Atlantis was dying!

But at least continents would be changed so that new lands would be born.

We required 10 minutes to reach a safety depth under the surface. We couldn't actually go higher because we didn't know whether the time-front had passed through yet or if perhaps straggling offshoots would be following.

"The time-wall's speed was high, Your Eminence," said Cunor. "It must have really gone away by now."

I staked all we had on one move. Although we would have been safer in the depths of the sea, we surfaced. The time-front had actually passed on but we were met with such a tidal wave that our craft became a helpless plaything of the giant billows. Only the highest mountain tops of Atlantis were still to be seen. I saw water wherever I looked. But there was no trace of the *Tosoma.*

Even the enemy ships had ceased their attacks. If their commanding officers had even a grain of sense they would have to know that there was nothing more here to destroy. That department was being adequately taken care of by the quakes and the terrible tidal waves.

We took the shaking and buffeting for 2 hours while I sent out uninterrupted calls on the craft's strong transmitter. High aloft, above and beyond the dark hurricane clouds, there was a far-outstretched light phenomenon. It couldn't be the sun because the sun was never in the North.

I knew what the scattering atomic fires of an exploded spaceship looked like but I didn't want to believe my eyes. Then the next overlap front came racing toward us.

Secretly broken-hearted, I gave the order to dive. My friends were no longer among the living.

150 ADVENTURES FROM NOW

It's a matter of Life &
Death from the Stars

8/ DEEPSLEEP

In 10 minutes I would be medically dead. According to instructions I lay loosely relaxed on the contour couch and listened to the soporific strains of hypno-music. Poised over my skull was the probe helmet of the pulsator. My normal vital rhythm was gradually slowing down.

Still to come was the automatic injection of preservative serum, a technique that my worthy race had known for a long time. Healthy subjects were able to survive biomedical deepsleep for more than 500 years entirely without harm. Life functions, such as metabolism, were reduced almost to zero.

The pressure dome had been fitted out with the necessary equipment. Formerly the installation had been on board a hospital ship belonging to my full squadron but we had transferred it here.

I relaxed my will completely in order to yield to the insinuating effects of the music. The time had come for me to retreat into the absolute calm and peace of deepsleep if I didn't want to lose my reason. I had become the loneliest living being on the planet.

It had taken about 4 months before the elements had subsided enough for us to even consider emerging to the surface. After that we had begun our long and futile search.

I had not been able to discover either Arkonide or native Atlantean. The protective fortresses and pyramid silos erected by Feltif still existed but the people had disappeared.

A sense of despair had driven Cunor and myself from place to place in senseless haste. We finally located life here & there but they were creatures of such a frightfully primitive state that we avoided making any contact with them. The barbarians of the icy North had been spared but our truly intelligent Atlanteans and the colonists in the East & West were no longer there. Either they had been killed by the mountainous tidal waves or they had been drawn up into the numerous time-fronts.

For 6 long months we had searched, sent out radio calls, searched some more and signaled again & again. Arkon appeared to have forgotten us completely. The irreplaceable radio stations of Atlantis and the 2 southern continents had been destroyed by the effects of enemy action. The transmitting capability of the undersea dome was comparatively weak and could never bridge the gulf between us and the home worlds. I came to regret not having installed a powerful, major class transmitter in the submarine stronghold. At the time it had seemed purposeless, since hyper-wave installations had no business being under the surface of the sea. The dome was supposed to be a refuge only—a provisional shelter on a shortime basis. Why should we install such large, space-consuming equipment when we needed every corner, so to speak, for the really vital installations?

So it was that we flew over every continent in the glider. The face of the 3d planet had changed. Great islands had sunk and new oceans had come into being. Among the sunken lands was Atlantis, which was only marked now by a small archipelago of islands that were actually the mountaintops.

Our pressure dome base of operations had finally come to rest at a depth of 9348 feet, which was more than 1500 fathoms below the surface.

Then, shortly before our time of final resignation, Lt. Cunor was struck down with a stone handaxe by a stupid barbarian of the North. I had stood dry-eyed over the grave of my last companion for a long time, finally flying away in a state of inexpressible weariness and exhaustion.

My one last measure of precaution was taken solely

on the basis of a stubborn ember of hope that still lay smouldering deep within me. At some time or another certainly somebody would have to investigate what had become of Admiral Atlan. Somewhere along the way someone would have to process—ergo, become aware of —the hypercom message I broadcasted shortly before the explosion of the *Paito*. Arkon was certainly not dead yet and after all I was a member of the ruling house.

On the basis of these considerations I mounted a small super-sensitive apparatus on the highest island mountain peak. Capable of reacting to disturbances such as a space-warp, it was designed to hail any chance spaceship coming out of transition within reasonable cosmic distances. In which case a relay transmitter would notify the robot brain in the sea dome and as a consequence I would be awakened at once from deep-sleep.

I had cautiously set the maximum limit of sleep for 500 years but was quite certain that my comrades would come before then, if only in a miserable courier cruiser.

So I had given myself over to the sleep couch with a certain sense of reassurance. It would have been senseless and dangerous to my mental health if I had waited day after day and night after night. In deepsleep time became negligible and my detector was reliable.

I became sleepy. Next to me stood my servant robot, a special model with which I could converse because of its excellent positronic brain.

"How long now, Rico?" I asked in a whisper.

"Immediately, Your Eminence, you will go to your rest at once," said the med-machine. This time I was not disturbed by the metallic timbre of its mechanical vocal cords.

"Go to rest?" I repeated hesitantly. "Rest—peace—freedom! From whom or what? My conscience?"

"Relax yourself, Eminence," came the insistent words from the mouth of the robot.

Fiery pinwheels began to spin before my vision. Suddenly I saw Tarth's deeply lined face. He smiled at me encouragingly. Then came Inkar, Cunor, Kosol, Cerbus and all the many friends whom I had driven to their deaths.

I wanted to cry out but couldn't. Why had I chosen to defend this world? Why?

"Rico, do you think an intelligent race will ever develop out of the barbarian survivors?"

"Relax, my prince—the time of sleep begins . . ."

Time!

I had underestimated it. I had overlooked the facts of time. That which was to follow would not be contaminated by the same mistakes. I swore it to myself and in the name of the Greater Empire and my revered ancestral house.

200 ADVENTURES FROM NOW
It's spooky adventure on the
World of the Disembodied

9/ REWARD ACROSS MILLENNIA

Someone was singing. He had a rich, beautiful voice. I listened with an increasing awareness while forgetting my painful headache. For a very long while I drank in these pleasing sounds.

When I opened my eyes I saw a dark-skinned young man sitting close to me. In his wonderful baritone he was singing "Home, home on the range . . ." Beyond him stood a dark-eyed officer who wore the insignia of a governing administrator. The young man with the dark complexion continued to sing. Then I recognized who he was. Lt. Fron Wroma belonged to the officers' staff of the Terranian super-battleship *Drusus.*

Suddenly somebody said: "I happened to remember that music or song has a beneficial effect on the nervous systems of your people."

I straightened up slowly in the lowered folding lounge, finally recalling the fact that I had been narrating under the influence of my auxiliary brain.

Perry Rhodan smiled at me.

Reginald Bell handed me a refreshing drink. While doing so, he spoke with an unaccustomed gentleness and thoughtfulness. "They finally showed up, Admiral, but they were a little late. However, the barbarians of your so-called Larsaf 3 have developed some, you might say. You didn't defend the Earth in vain, Atlan. And those that came after you will not ever make the same mistake again."

I nodded mutely. It was difficult to switch one's train of thought so suddenly into the present.

They let me take my time, until Rhodan asked: "That alarm mechanism—wouldn't you say it failed to function during that period?"

I shook my head. "No, it was in perfect operating condition but no spaceships appeared during that time. I continued to awaken at intervals of 500 years. Finally I had a look around outside but the Terranians hadn't progressed very much. In order to conquer my loneliness I always went back down into the sea dome. When I was awakened for the 21st time I found that there was on Earth a great civilization known as the Roman Empire. Unfortunately my awakening came a bit late because I had slept through the Grecian culture. From that time on I remained 'above' but there was still no possibility of summoning a spaceship. I had to wait a long time, Perry!"

The machinery of the *Drusus* was in operation. I lifted my head to listen. "A wonderful sound, that—almost as beautiful as Wroma's voice," I said quietly. "It was a good idea to have him sing. I love that ancient song that they used to sing in the United States. It's been a long time . . ."

The *Drusus* took off. The synthetic planet Wanderer fell away from us. It was then that I firmly resolved to explain my mistakes to humans as clearly as possible. Perhaps they could learn from them. Besides, I now knew whom I had been fighting back there 10,000 years ago.

The uncanny creatures from the other time-plane were called Druufs. I looked across at Rhodan. He sat calmly in the commander's seat in front of the countless controls of the flying titan of space.

This time I would not have to wait for reinforcements of ships and materials, most assuredly not! That man

over there, whose primitive forefathers had killed my last companion, would demand satisfaction for the near destruction of a world that he called Terra.

I decided to retire to my cabin.

Fron Wroma smiled at me. "Transition in 10 minutes, sir," he called out. "Then we'll be home again."

Home . . . How strange it sounded. I mentally savored the concept. The armorplated bulkhead doors of the Command Central opened automatically. The cell activator beat gently against my chest. It had kept the promise of an unknown benefactor.

I left them to themselves, these curiously likable barbarians. So it had been rewarding, after all, to defend Larsaf 3. Some of the natives survived because we had been able to divert and disperse some of the overlap front with the impulse cannons.

It had actually been worth it!

I had relived the traumatic last days of Atlantis, now I looked forward to the dramatic new days of action in space, time and the dimensions with the Peacelord of the Solar Empire.

250 ADVENTURES FROM NOW
You'll be struck by
Operation: Lightning

THE SHIP OF THINGS TO COME

PERRY RHODAN gives a command.

Maj. Clyde Ostal, an experienced officer of the Solar Security Service, is to take Responsibility for the armed spacer *Tigris*. His mission, together with 31 picked men: to leave Earth in the ship in a deliberate attempt to learn whether the Robot Regent of Arkon can detect the frequencies of structural compensators and thereby determine the position of spaceships going thru hypertransition.

In 2042 the Positronicon that rules the Arkonide Empire does not yet know the location of Earth—and Perry Rhodan wants to keep it that way. Hence, Maj. Ostal's important mission.

You're in for a wild time when—

THE *TIGRIS* LEAPS
By
Kurt Brand

500 ADVENTURES FROM NOW
Perhaps you'll quail at
The Voices of Qual

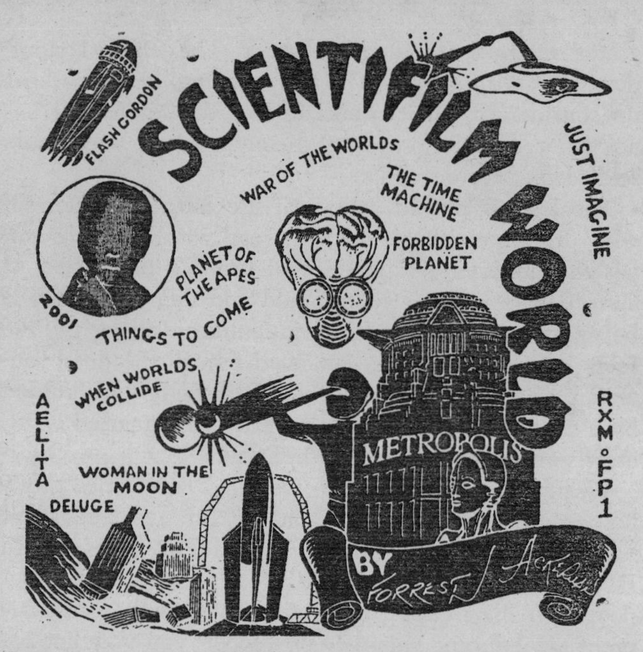

THE INVASION OF THE SAUCER-MEN, 1957, was based on an original short story by sf author Paul W. Fairman, "The Cosmic Frame", published in the May 1955 *Amazing Stories*. I quote myself from a review of the time:

As the picture's in conventional black & white you'll have to take the dialog's word for it that the little men are actually green but little they definitely are, being a quartet of Hollywood's dwarves. Made up with Lorre-like eyes bulging from macrocephalic heads, the 4 bulbous-brained interplanetarians represent a sinister threat to the townfolk (especially teenfolk) of a small American community.

It's a pretty good little film. Unpretentious, it spins an almost "homey" little yarn whose mood is a well-integrated mixture of humor & horror. The original story, downbeat with a tragic O. Henry ending, has been beat up considerably in its translation to the screen but has not suffered in the process and emerges as an acceptable sci-fi comedy cum chills.

The lead is played by a real life fan, Steve Terrell, who, driving on a dark & lonely road with his girlfriend, has the unnerving experience of running over what at first appears to be a young child and then turns out to be an extraterrestrial. In as gruesome a scene as I've seen in a scientifilm, the mangled arm of the dead saucerian detaches itself from the alien's body and, guided by a single unwinking orb attached to its gnarled wrist, crawls away—to menace another day.

Wasn't it Jack Williamson who had aeroplanes growing on trees in "Dragon's Island"? Strange things are happening and the spirit of Charles Fort survives. In INVASION OF THE SAUCER-MEN the saucerites put people in their cups by injecting them with about 200 proof alcohol; and this they do (sober, you may not believe this; but I swear it by Arthur Clarke's Moon) by extendable natural growths at their claw-tips which do not resemble but *are* hypodermic needles!

Not since the surrealistic CHIEN ANDALOU has there been such a gory scene involving an eyeball as when one of the saucer-men gets an orb gouged out in a bloody battle with a long-horned bull.

But from the clever cartoons that accompany the credits at the beginning of the picture to the final shriek that closes it, Eddie Cahn directed with chetongueek (tongue-in-cheek) and the laffs balance the fright-induced epidermal subthermal lumps.

Shock Short

You'll find a surprise in store in—

DEATH IN STORE

by

Dale Hammell
(A PR Discovery)

The ship lay on the surface, silvery and steel-blue against the tanned soil. Bent nearly in two, the cruiser was cracked and shattered. Invisible seams had split. Razor-sharp shards of acrylic and metal were strewn about the landscape. All through the day the ship was silent, still.

That night the crew of the ship awoke from unconsciousness. Thin beams of white light shone over the shadowed landscape. Hauntingly beautiful. The spacemen waited patiently for the dawn.

With morning's light they discovered their ship had sunk into the soil. They stood for a moment, glycerine tears running down their polymer-protected faces.

Everywhere grew up long gnarled, bent fibers. They blocked the few cleared paths. They almost completely obliterated the sky.

The ground, soft and porous, made hiking difficult.

The 6 figures pushed on through the dense jungle-like growths. Occasionally they came across various-sized patches of pulpy brown soil. As deadly as quicksand, they were constantly avoided by the party.

The air whistled as their acrylic-edged, vibratory machetes hacked away at the foliage. The air was cool, almost refrigerated, but large beads of perspiration formed on their foreheads. Their protective polymer skins were soon discarded. Sweat ran down their faces, stinging their eyes and dripping off perfectly sculpted noses. Their bodysuits, heavy with the salty liquid, were also discarded. Their hair, sea green, clung to their heads parasitically. Heavy boots and gloves hid swollen painful blisters.

Ahead and to the left of them there suddenly appeared, in a well-rounded depression, a pool of clean clear cool water. The tension that had been enveloping each member of the party broke. They started cutting furiously at the barring growths. Their laughter rang out in great waves. They were a bunch of frolicking school boys. They were grateful men.

One member, the last man, ran forward past the others, his naked body smudged with sweat, eyes glazed, mouth frothing. Groping and tripping, he forced himself through the scratching, tearing fibers, towards the water. The others realizing it too late, shouted, warned him.

Unknowingly the crazed man ran headlong into a patch of the deadly soil, acres wide and twice as long. Before the others could reach him to even try to help him, he sank, like the ship, out of sight, screaming . . .

"Here, Mrs. Mortimer, let me exchange this for another one. This peach has a BIG BROWN BRUISE on it!" smiled the tall freckle-faced clerk at the produce counter of the corner Supermarket.

600 ADVENTURES FROM NOW
You'll hold your breath at
Pucky's Peril in Hyperspace

Our Smashing Serial in the Doc Smith Vein

NEW LENSMAN

By
William B. Ellern

Part 2

CHAPTER 3

KIDNAPPED

Lt. McQueen found the Security Division. The receptionist directed him to Col. Hanovich's office. Hanovich's secretary told him that he was expected. She ushered the Lieutenant into Col. Hanovich's office and closed the door firmly behind him when he was inside.

The open curtains along one wall of the Director of Security's office revealed a window looking out into the Dome, a hemisphere a half mile in diameter hollowed out of the center of the crater wall. In the center of the Dome, held in place by tractor and pressor beams, was the artificial sun giving out light and warmth to the inhabitants. The Dome was ringed with commercial enterprises, and housed the park. The City Hall of Copernicus was part of the Dome's wall. Indeed, each "building" of Copernicus was a set of rooms hollowed out of the rock surrounding a pair of shafts from the travel level. The travel tunnels emptied into the Dome. The Dome was the center of activity of both Copernicus and of the whole moon. Only recently was it possible to economically create other domes on the moon. Still the Dome would remain unique, for soon mankind would come out of hiding on the moon. This was to happen later, when whole craters became cities roofed with the Rodebush-Bergenholm field. Impervious to meteor storms.

Col. Owen Hanovich came around his desk and shook hands. He was a somewhat stout man with red hair, a bushy red beard and a black glove on his left hand.

"Welcome, Lt. McQueen," he said, eyes twinkling. "It's not often that a Sector Chief of the Triplanetary Service visits us. Sit down."

The Lieutenant sat down and asked, "What makes you think I'm a Sector Chief in the Triplanetary Service?"

"I was aboard the spaceship *Edwardium Rex* during the Coventry Affair."

"Oh, a passenger?"

"Yes. Sometimes it does seem unfortunate that the penalty for piracy is death, but then, if we let every attractive woman go . . ." Hanovich trailed off into a moment's silence.

"She's still around. The jury let her go."

"Oh?"

"I'm on a spy hunt now. You've been checked and apparently you aren't one of the opposition, so I'll give you the details of what has been discovered so far. First, however, is this room secure?"

Hanovich slid one of the writing surfaces in his desk out, rotated it and examined the lights embedded inside. "Yes," he said, "everything is in order. The shields and blocks are up."

"How often are they maintained?"

Col. Hanovich's eyebrows darkened. "Maintained?"

He took this as a clue. "My office is checked every week. We have our own group to maintain the correct operation of these devices in the Security Department and in the City Hall in general. I might add that the members of the group have been in the department for at least 10 years. Each is an expert on bugs, taps and snoops."

"The window?"

"One way vilar. It looks like part of the wall from the outside. A new material."

"I know. Pull the drapes," Larry said. "Vilar is also transparent in the UV region. It takes some special equipment but the Service has already had occasion to look through it. Anything we can do, we should expect the opposition to be able to do."

Hanovich pulled the drapes and Larry continued.

"As a result of the meeting of the Board of Directors, we have reason to suspect that John Griffin is either one of, or at least in contact with, the unknown agency which the Patrol . . . er . . . the Service is investigating. Mayor Love is checking into Director Griffin's activities."

"I know," Col. Hanovich said, with just a trace of smugness in his voice. "Here is a copy of the results of the Mayor's efforts. He's turned the problem over to my division and I was just about to put a team to work doing a detailed check of the files and records of all the people the Mayor came up with."

Larry read through the brief report and then put it back on Hanovich's desk.

"The man mentioned in my department is in the Watchman/Traffic Control Section. Here." Under the clear surface of Hanovich's desk were pictures of each of the men on public security duty. Hanovich pointed to one of the pictures. "This is what he looks like."

Larry leaned forward and looked at the man. The

face was neither distinctive nor familiar. "OK, how about the five men who dropped out of sight?"

"Nothing yet. Obviously they eat, so any excess purchases of food by anyone in the group will eventually lead us to them. On the other hand, they could have left Copernicus through some secret exit, though I don't know of any. No one has been reported missing but that doesn't mean that these people couldn't be impersonating someone without close friends or relationships."

"The primary thing that bothers me is that for several months now these agents have had free run of Copernicus," Larry said. "What have they done in that time? What listening devices or booby traps have they set? They have taken the time and trouble to infiltrate the Facilities Division. Why? What's their reason? What's their schedule? What's going to blow up in our faces at a critical moment? And most important, how are we going to find out?"

"Since the start of the Jovian Wars we've dealt with problems similar to these," Hanovich said, as though it was of no great importance. "As an initial measure Security has a 'Customs Section', which checks and records all of the baggage, personal effects and goods being shipped or brought into Copernicus. We try to stop anything potentially dangerous. From the customs records we should be able to determine what kind of electronic equipment or anything else they brought in."

"Not necessarily," Larry said with a smile. "I'm a perambulating warehouse of equipment and I doubt that you have any idea what all I'm carrying. It all looks innocent."

Hanovich looked pleased, like a cat with a mouth full of canary. "What's it got in its pocketsis?" he hissed.

Larry smiled, catching the reference to one of the few enduring classics of English literature.

Hanovich typed a key phrase into the keyboard on his desk. He thought a moment, typed in additional information and then read from the plate. "Goggles, binoculars, wristwatch, pocket chronometer, belt communicator, flashlight, automatic lighter, wallet, change, a money belt, a pocket knife and a knife in your boot heel. And the goggles. I admit that every spaceship officer I've ever seen wears them but I've never seen them use them for anything except as sunglasses. Care to explain?"

"The goggles and binoculars form part of the traditional uniform," Larry answered. "The goggles come from the First Jovian War when they were used as eye protection from atomic explosion and laser radiation. The originals had a semi-opaque liquid driven between the lenses by an explosive charge, when a certain intensity or type of light hit a sensor on them. The modern ones use a high speed, reversible, light intensity limiting effect; phototropism it's called. Of course neither item is required unless you're using direct viewports. You still haven't mentioned a large part of the stuff I'm carrying."

Hanovich looked even more pained, if that was possible.

"At least you have a record of their possessions, even if we aren't sure what those possessions really are," Larry said. "If we can account for everything, that's a good start."

"I'll put a team to work on that point."

"You might put one team to work just watching these people. Warn them that we're not playing polite parlor games. This one is for keeps. An error, and they will know we are onto them. That could be fatal to us all! Handle them with care, and remember that we may not have all of them spotted. Matter of fact, keep looking for other connections and other groups. We need information desperately!" Larry said, getting up. "I've got to go now. I'll check with you later."

"Alright. I hope we'll have something for you nextime we meet. You're staying at the New Frontier Hotel?"

"Yes."

"We'll contact you there if we find out anything important. Or better yet," Hanovich reached into his desk and brought out what appeared to be a coin, "carry this and we'll be able to trace you and contact you wherever you are in Copernicus."

"Thanks, but they may be aware of your finder. If they are, I'd rather they weren't able to follow me so easily. Thanks anyway."

Biding the Director of Security goodby, Lt. McQueen left the City Hall and started through the Dome toward his hotel.

Wherever the men of Tellus go, they try to take part of their planet with them. Be it the farthest point of the universe man has explored, a wilderness of timeless rock soaking in endless vacuum or the midst of magma and ash of a planet not quite born—there is always a cave or bubble or dome to which the men there could point and say, "There! That's like home! That's the way it was!" Nowhere is this more evident than on the moon. The Dome had been carved from lifeless rock in the heart of a crater wall. Even after its half mile hemisphere had been cut and laboriously carted out of the crater wall, there was no life there. Nothing could live in the airless, rock-bound darkness. Air and water were wrung from the rock of the moon. Some of the pulverized remains of the yet dark dome was mixed with micro-organisms from Tellus, brought there to create a nutrient soil. There was air and water and soil.

Now. Let there be light! Man created, out of his own need, a miniature sun to hang in the center of the Dome. It had been changed many times before Lt. Larry McQueen's eyes first saw it. The first suns were cold and gave out only light. Even now part of the heat was produced by power generators underneath the Dome. The sun that hung in the sky of the Dome now was the right size, shape and color. It gave out heat and light and that special something called "friendliness". It was part of a single, almost endless spring day, in an Eden created by man, with night coming only once a year just before Founders Day. Underneath that friendly sun grew a park, with walkways bordered in grass. Trees grew from what was once sterility. Each green thing carefully watched, cherished and nurtured into life. The heart of the wall of the crater named Copernicus was alive and it was hoped would remain that way.

Now the Dome was a commonplace thing to its inhabitants. It was part of the accepted order of things. Only the tourists came, looked and wondered. The walkways were filled with people, many on important business, not sensing the beauty around them. Some annoyed that they had to walk through the park. Yet here and there, there were a few. Walking for the enjoyment of it. Enjoying the beauty of something that was not Earth but *of* Earth. To some an Earth they had never visited. An Earth so close, yet an eternity of night away.

Lt. McQueen entered the Dome, walking as rapidly as possible across it toward the New Frontier Hotel. He was considering the conversation he had just had with Col. Hanovich. He was trying to decide whether he had said or implied too much. Whether he should leave Griffin and company in the local Security Division's hands or go to work on the problem himself. He needed information on who was represented by the black spaceship. Where did it come from? What was its purpose? Did Griffin have this information? How to get it out of him? The Mayor he liked and respected. If the Mayor were still working on the problem, he wouldn't worry. Hanovich . . . hmm. Perhaps it was just a conflict of interest. He'd give him a day and see what Security came up with. He had a feeling that Hanovich was the type of individual too busy playing games with words to *do* anything.

Something was wrong!

The impression intruded itself on Larry's thoughts and brought him out of them into the world around him. He had walked almost halfway to his destination while trying to decide on the proper manner of handling Hanovich. The walkway bent in a long curve toward the hotel. A lot of trees here. Around him were several men, all apparently going in the same direction. Ahead was a four-wheeled, electric cargo hauler and beyond that a policeman. What was wrong? He didn't recognize any of the people around him. Larry slowed a little. A couple of the men moved on past but some of the rest slowed too. Larry reached for his belt communicator.

"Pardon me, but . . ." A voice came from in back of him. A hand touched his shoulder and everything faded into blackness.

The man who had touched him watched as the lieutenant crumpled to the sidewalk. He pretended surprise and pointed at Larry with one hand, while the other one, which had touched McQueen, dropped an instrument into his side pocket.

"What happened?" he asked the man next to him.

Several other people came up to join those around the unconscious Solarian Patrolman. The policeman came running up. Larry would have recognized him as the man whose picture Hanovich had pointed out. He knelt over Larry for a moment, then stood up, pulled a communicator from his belt and said into it in a loud voice, "Ambulance."

As if by magic, right on cue, down the pathway came an enclosed white ambulance hauler with two men in white jackets on board. Lt. McQueen was put inside. The doors closed. The policeman stepped on the back platform and the ambulance left.

* * * *

The first person to miss Lt. McQueen was Mayor Love. He had been considering Griffin's reaction to the word Icarus, and it bothered him. He wanted to discuss the matter with the lieutenant. Larry had given him the channel and selective call number of his belt communicator. Ron called it through the Copernicus communication system. There was no answer. Puzzled, the Mayor waited a few minutes and tried again. No answer. He asked the system to send a coded "pulse back" command, which would make McQueen's communicator send back a pulse if it was within receiving range. No answer.

Still puzzled, the Mayor considered what to do next. Lt. McQueen was going to see Col. Hanovich. The Mayor called the Director of Security, who told him that Larry had left a little while earlier for his hotel. The Mayor called the hotel and discovered that Lt. McQueen had checked out. No messages had been left and no destination had been given.

Now the Mayor was really puzzled. Where was he? The Central File computer indicated that Larry was still in the city. What set of circumstances could occur that he would check out of the hotel and disappear? The Mayor looked at his watch. An hour, and the "day" would be over. He decided to allow that much time before alerting anyone that something might have happened to Lt. McQueen.

An hour later the Mayor again tried to contact Larry. He tried the local office of the Solarian Patrol. Larry had cautioned him about it because it was suspected of being "porous". The field office didn't even know who Lt. McQueen was.

That left Security. Mayor Love called Hanovich and explained what had happened. Hanovich listened without comment, requested that the Mayor not spread the news, and promised to check.

When Col. Hanovich broke the connection, he swore to himself softly. "And he told *me* to be careful! I hope there's something to rescue when we find him," he said, and then added as an afterthought, "if we ever do . . ."

Hanovich checked the team of "watchers" and discovered that they had not yet found everyone they were to watch. Disappointed, he settled back to wait.

COSMICLUBS
for
RHOFANS
PUCKYFANS
ATLANFANS

SOMETHING NEW has been added!

The 1st ATLAN FAN CLUB!

The Leader of the Fans For Atlan group is P. CHARLES LABBE and he says, "I've the hopes of eventually putting out an ATLAN fanzine." If Atlantean blood flows in your veins (and there's a simple test to tell: just prick your finger and if you bleed purple with polkadots there's no doubt about your Atlantean ancestry. However, you must observe very closely because within 1 millisecond after being exposed to the air the blood camouflages itself and turns red like an ordinary Earth mortal)—if Atlantean blood flows in your veins you'll want to write P. Charles Labbe for membership in his Atlan Fan Club at 174 Lemay Rd., Woonsocket/RI 02895. If you're local, he'll welcome your call at (401) 769-0748.

NEW Clubs for Rhofans are helmed by:

TIM CURRAN
67 Gould St.
Wakefield/MASS 01880

BRUCE SEALY
617 Dover Dr.
Richardson
Dallas/TX 75080

LOU PERKINS *
388 SPS, Box 2957
APO SF 96288

CLUBS PREVIOUSLY ANNOUNCED

MIKE BOTELHO
157 Field St.
New Bedford/MASS 02740

RICHARD ABRAMS
R#1 Box 137
Plainsville/IN 47568

BEN RASKIN
5610 W. 75 Terrace
Prairie Village/KS 66208

BERTRAND SZÖGHY
3105 P. Montreus
Sainte-Foy
Quebec, 10, P.Q.
CANADA G1W-3A1

DAVID FLAME
8100 Pennhill Rd.
Elkins Park/PA 19177

BETH BOULES
2421 Westport Dr.
Dayton/OH 45406

* LOU is located in Thailand and says, "Mine is a fan club aimed at Rhofans in the military. There are bound to be a lot of us (I am in the Air Force myself) and if others are willing I don't see why we shouldn't have our own club. Perhaps together we can deal with distribution problems within our exchange system (I have only once seen PERRY RHODAN in a PX). If others are interested they can write me and I'll act as a clearing house for ideas on how our club should be run until we really get started. Yours till the Regent short-circuits."

KEVIN HENNESSEY
"THE NEW POWER"
36 Payson Rd.
Cornwall-on-Hudson
NY 12520

STEVEN GUTTERMAN
21440 Westhampton
Oak Park/MI 48237

SHARON STEFL
604 So. Kenilworth
Oak Park/IL 60304

BRIAN E. NEVISH
"THE TECHNICORPS"
Sunrise Hills Rd. 1
Industry/PA 15052

PERRY RHODAN FAN
CLUB OF BOULDER
DAVID O. ANDERSON
555 Clover Lane
Boulder/CO 80303

ECKHARD GERDES
Pucky Fan Club
(with fanzine)
2909 Colfax St.
Evanston/IL 60201

ATTENTION All Club Leaders. If you wish YOUR CLUB to be included in the NEXT LIST to be published, you must NOW drop a postcard so stipulating to FORRY RHODAN 2495 Glendower Ave., Hollywood/CA 90027.

JOEL SPENCER of 2506 - 45 St., Rock Island / IL 61201 says:

I have read enough scientifiction to know the good stuff from the bad stuff. And boy, you guys are great! I also write science fiction. Look for my new book coming out in about a year or so. It's called "Creation of the Cosmos II". I picked up #32 and read it in 2 days time. I subscribed 10 minutes later. I also went into debt for subscribing. What I don't do to read PERRY RHODAN!

MRS. R. J. REIS is seeking a cell-shower, price no object:

Sob! sob! Just finished #52 and to my sorrow saw the number of PRs already written in German. Could you possibly arrange for me to have that longevity treatment that PR took? Here I am already 53 years old and at the present rate of issues I'm afraid I won't live long enough to read the entire series.

I'm afraid I've been "hooked" on the series. It's not often that I find reading material that I can say I want to read & reread. I have the entire ERBurroughs & the Lensman series plus a few others that I go back and reread once or twice a year. Outside of Andre Norton I find very few of the books written today worth the effort of bringing home! I'd truly like to shut myself up in FJA's library for a reading orgy! I do hope you can keep up the work of editing the series and that your wife can keep on translating.

BRYAN MOUNCER is short & zonk:

I think anybody that doesn't like PERRY RHODAN books is completely donk. Shantel for bringing Perry to America.

PAULA FRIEDRICH addresses "My Favorite Editors":

I really don't know whether to *laugh* or *cry*! I just recently received my mail order copies of PR from Kris Darkon and when I read the Perryscopes I gathered that PR may go *4* a month; well, I thought, I couldn't ask for a better surprise. Pure joy & solid contentment set off fireworks in my head, which were swiftly quenched by a bucket of water—in other words, by my tears when I realized I could only *pay* for 2 a month. You see, I buy a lot of other books too and am trying to complete my Lensman and Conan series, so I lack an excess of cash. Maybe I should forget those other books? (*Seems like the only sensible solution, under the circumstances.*)

If you ever cut out even *1* feature of PR, I shall tear your name out of all my PR books. (*Krosh! If it would make you* that *cross we wouldn't think of doublecrossing you!*)

WALLACE DILLON of 512 E. 5 St., Laurel/MS 39440 addresses "Dear 4SJ":

After reading PR #51, Return from the Void, I had to write. I almost flaked MY snow when I read about the Brain turning over 75% of its fleet to Perry. I now think Perry and the gang are getting the respect they deserve. I think the Brain realized that if it had to fight the Solar Imperium it would lose. If anyone gets the control of the Arkonide Empire it must be Perry.

I've been a fan hooked on Perry ever since ENTERPRISE STARDUST came out. Perry is the greatest thing to happen to science fiction since the invention of the time machine. The only gripe I have about PR is when I hear someone cut down Perry. If they don't like it they don't have to buy it. Just leave the book on the shelf. Someone who really appreciates Perry will come and buy it. How can anyone cut down Perry when he is the "Alpha & Omega" of science fiction?

BARNABY RAPOPORT, Noxon Rd., Lagrangeville/ NY 12540 makes an unusual contribution:

I haven't written to PR in a long time mainly because I've been diverting my letterhack energies toward submitting my fiction to assorted markets and I thought your readers would enjoy a little piece of fantasy which is, to my knowledge, the shortest of its breed. Hope you enjoy it!

THE WORLD'S SHORTEST FANTASY STORY
By
Barnaby Rapoport

"Abracadabra!"
Poof!
"Meow?"

(*Had you ever considered retitling this story* AbraCATabra? *Or* CATastrophe? *Would you like to see how it would look translated into the Tongue of Tomorrow, Esperanto the Universalanguage?*

"Abrakadabra!"
Puf!
"Miau?"

Remember, when this masterpiece in miniature wins the Pulitzer Prize and the Ann Radcliffe Award, you read it here first!)

PS: If any payment is forthcoming, donate to your fund for your new collection housing/museum. (*Thank you! We took $50 out of one pocket and put it in the other. Of course, this also bought Movie Rights and an option on developing the plot into a 3-year daily afternoon TV soap opera. Sell a lot of catfood!*)

Only room for a small portion of a welcome letter from regular contributor HENRY DAVIS JR. of Baker Station Rd., Goodlettsville/TN. Perhaps the rest of the letter nextime.

Scientifilm World was very good. I remember seeing the movie itself (THE MAN FROM PLANET X) and I enjoyed it very much. Planet X itself reminded me of my idea of the planet Pluto.

"Racial Memory" seemed to span thousands of years. However, there was nothing primitive about the theme at all. Superb.

Other than I think you spelled the author's name wrong (*how so?*) I could find nothing wrong with "Under the Lavender Skies". Let's just hope that the astronauts never really land there.

"Alien Catastrophe" almost was, but not quite. Somebody's been feeding the Sqirgl nuts in the park.

"Cop Out" seemed a flop out even tho I sympathize with the theme of the story. If other planets are inhabited, I doubt if they even know the meaning of the word morals.

SPYBOT should be one of the best PR since AGAIN: ATLAN.

Address Fanmail To
FJA: THE PERRYSCOPE
2495 Glendower Ave.
Hollywood/CA 90027

AVOID THAT "SINKING SENSATION"

THE ATLANTEANS *couldn't* avoid that sinking sensation.

But you can.

No more do you have to go to the drugstore or newsstand or supermarket and be disappointed to find somebody's beat you to the current PERRY RHODAN.

Perry will gladly pilot himself right to your mailbox.

6 copies in the next 3 months for $6.75 ppd.

$13.50 ppd. for the next half year, a whole dozen copies.

Or you could get lucky like long-time subscriber LINDA HANER, young reader of Galena, Ks., and find, thru random selection, that you're the happy winner of the MONTHLY DOUBLE. Lucky Linda gets TWENTY-FOUR COPIES for her 12 issue subscription.

You May Be Next!

Money Order or Check (write nothing on the back of either) to:

KRIS DARKON
2495 Glendower Ave.
Hollywood/CA 90027

Convenient Coupon provided on Next Page

PERRY RHODAN #63 thru..

NAME (Print Clearly) ....

(AGE) ....

ST. ADDRESS, POB or RFD ....

CITY ....

STATE (Spell Out) ....

ZIP ....

COUNTRY ....